ELFSONG

ALSO BY ANN TURNER

Grass Songs

Grasshopper Summer

One Brave Summer

Nettie's Trip South

Dakota Dugout

Rosemary's Witch

ELFSONG

ANN TURNER

HARCOURT BRACE & COMPANY

San Diego   New York   London

Requests for permission to make copies of any part of the work should be
mailed to: Permissions Department, Harcourt Brace & Company,
6277 Sea Harbor Drive, Orlando, Florida 32887-6777.

Library of Congress Cataloging-in-Publication Data
Turner, Ann Warren.
Elfsong / Ann Turner.
p.   cm.
"Jane Yolen books."
Summary: When ten-year-old Maddy Trevor goes for her annual summer
visit to her grandfather and her cat Sabrina goes missing, she
searches the woods and discovers a magical world.
ISBN 0-15-200826-8
[1. Elves—Fiction. 2. Music—Fiction. 3 Cats—Fiction.
4. Grandfathers—Fiction.] I. Title.
PZ7.T8535El   1995
[Fic]—dc20   95-2251

Illustration copyright © 1995 by David Christiana
The text was set in Kennerly.
Designed by Lisa Peters

First edition
A B C D E
Printed in the United States of America

To my dear friends
Lauren Mills and Dennis Nolan,

with love

ELFSONG

The Beginning

Everything has a name.

Everything has a song.

Elves hear all the songs of the world, and animals, birds, and other creatures hear pieces of the songs of the world. Humans hear none of these notes, only the slightest, faintest traces of their whispers. Which they call wind. Which they call water.

Long ago, when elves and people were friends, mankind heard more of the songs of the world. Then the world was young and green; unicorns, elves, great eagles, and

1

hunters roamed the world. There was no enmity between elves and humans. Certain elf families were linked with human families, down through the generations. And they helped one another.

But then people began to use the elves. To want their magic for themselves, so that their farms would grow bigger, so their wealth would increase, so they would be more important and live longer. Then elves took to the hills, and humans saw them no more. This is why the people did not see the great exodus five hundred years ago, when the elves built tight skin coracles and braved the high waves to come to this country.

They settled in the thick forests of the East, finding the lighter patches of shade and forging a new life there. Only deer and birds saw. Sometimes the people who lived at the edge of the forest, russet skinned with sharp eyes and old souls, saw the elves and wove stories about them. But the settlers who came to this land never believed such tales.

The first elves harvested the forest. They ate blueberries at the edge, and partridgeberries. They dug cattails from the swamps and collected the bright yellow pollen in spring, carrying it back to their dwellings in tightly woven grass baskets. From the pollen they made a golden bread called *lelan*, which they used for journeys, although no elf likes to be far from home for long. An elf could travel a whole day on one thin slice.

In the fall, when the time came for the *In-gathering*, they harvested acorns to store in covered baskets. In their birch-bark lodges, as the light lessened and cold crept in, they insulated the walls with cattail fluff and decorated deerskin robes with intricate colored designs. Wrapped in their ancient magic signs, elves gathered around fires and told tales. Elves who had been out traveling in the forest brought back new stories, sometimes telling of other elf colonies along winding rivers or in the desert, sometimes telling of disturbances in the eastern mountains that might have been the work of dwarves.

Young elves ready for adulthood took part in the ceremony of the *Crossing Over*. Marriages were made, which they called *Joinings*. Babies were started, gardens planned for the spring. The long story sagas, *Mildas,* were recorded in runes burned into thin scrolls of birch bark. These were the elves' greatest treasure, and were kept in a special lodge called the House of Scrolls, along with all the histories of life in the old land. So things continued for hundreds of years.

But in this year, in one forest in the East, there was a shadow over the planting in the spring, over elves' hopes for a peaceful life of celebrating and naming nature. For He had come back. There had always been owls in their woods, and the elves had made an uneasy pact with most of them. Frequent offerings of plump moles kept them silent. But not this one. Some years ago He had carried off two elves and devoured them. The songs of the elves and their sharp spears and arrows had driven Him off—but not for good. Having once tasted it, He had a hunger for elf blood, for *hislin*.

Sala, the leader of the eastern forest elves, said it was the same owl who had killed before. He could be identified by the twisted ear tuft on the left side of His face, and a particularly loud scream when hunting, a scream that made the elves shiver in their moss beds.

All of the other animals listened to the elves' calls and songs. But not this one. He was back to hunt them, and no elf could feel safe again until He was finally killed.

CHAPTER ONE

Maddy stood on the train platform. It was a familiar August ritual, this visit to her beloved grandpa. Smells assaulted her—the sharp diesel of the train, the hot metal of the wheels, the smell of cement and dust. A gritty wind blew Mother's hair across her face, and she coughed.

Mother reached out to hug Maddy. "Good-bye, have a good visit with Grandpa, don't stay up too late at night, remember to eat your vitamins in the morning, and"—she paused uncertainly—"have fun."

I will, Maddy thought. *We'll eat large bowls of salad for supper and take long walks in the woods. Later we will lie on a blanket to watch the stars, and Grandpa will tell me stories of Icarus, Pegasus, and the Greek gods who once lived on Olympus. And,* she thought, *each night Sabrina will sleep by my side.*

"Good-bye." Daddy gave her a quick hug and smiled. Maddy wondered if he was disappointed in her, that she wasn't going to music camp like her friend Emily. Her parents had asked if she wanted to go, but she'd said no. She didn't want to play that kind of music; she wanted *her* kind of music. She had tried taking lessons, but it had never worked. All those black notes marching over the crisp white paper made her head swim. *Her* music would be like a whale's song, looping up and down in great swoops of sound. Or like wolves, she thought, fingering her collar. She wished she could play music with long howls and sharp yaps of delight like wolves greeting each other.

"Good-bye." Maddy climbed the steps, turned at the top, and said in a dignified voice, "I hope your playing goes well, and I hope your tomatoes grow." A vague feeling of sadness settled in her chest.

The whistle shrieked. Maddy sat down on a greasy seat opposite a thin, faded woman and peered out the window. Daddy and Mother stood on the platform, waving. Maddy felt like giving a wolf howl, she was suddenly so lonely.

Jumping up, she thrust her head out the window. "Careful of your hands, Daddy. Don't work too hard. Remember what the doctor said!"

He nodded and waved cheerfully at her, waggling his fingers in the air as if to say, See, they're all right, don't worry. She blew a kiss to him, but imagined that kiss floating past the concrete platform and disappearing under the train's wheels. It would never find its way to Daddy's cheek.

The train jerked, once, twice. Her parents' faces slid out of view, and the dark colors of abandoned buildings took their place. *Abandoned, the way I feel each time they leave for a concert tour.* Was that why this year she had started to dislike the music her parents played—because it took them away? One day she had turned every silver picture frame to the wall in her living room. Each one marked a special moment in Mother or Daddy's life with music—a moment *she* was not in.

Maddy sighed and leaned back, knowing that if Mother were here she'd say, "Maddy! Don't put your head on that seat. Goodness knows how dirty it is!"

Maddy almost smiled. Grandpa wouldn't mind. He wouldn't even notice if her hair were greasy or smelled odd. *He will wait for me on the train platform,* Maddy thought. *He will be tall and thin with white wizard's hair. He will buy me ice cream, as always, and ask me about my year.*

I will say it was good and bad, and then we will drive up the hill to Grandpa's house. First I will smell the giant sunflowers. Then we will eat raspberries from a blue bowl. Then I will sleep with my face in Sabrina's black fur, and I will feel at home.

Chapter Two

There he was, all six feet of him, waiting like a statue on the platform. He was at the head of the line with one arm raised. He knew Maddy grew nervous if she couldn't see him right away.

She leapt off the steps, and he swept her up in a tight hug. "There!" He smoothed her hair back and set her down, grasping her hand. It reminded her that no one else in her life held her as tightly as Grandpa did.

"Good trip, pumpkin?" They walked briskly to a kiosk

and got their ice-cream cones; always vanilla for Maddy, always strawberry for Grandpa.

"OK," Maddy said, scooping the ice cream up in great bites. Mother ate in little bites, to make it last. Daddy ate in middle bites, like the mama bear in the Goldilocks story. Grandpa ate carefully and steadily, but for all his care, his mustache always turned pink.

"You're like a cow eating grass!" Maddy teased him.

"Certainly not like a cow. A dog, perhaps, one of the nice kinds with tiny teeth and a friendly smile." Arms touching, they walked to the car.

"Or a cat," said Maddy. "Emily has a cat that's so fat they have to take the food away and hide it. Is Sabrina ever like that?"

Grandpa licked his mustache clean. "No, she gets taken care of too well to be greedy. I think people are only greedy when they're not properly taken care of." They rounded the corner and found Grandpa's blue station wagon.

"Are you feeling greedy?" He did not look at her as they got in the car, but Maddy knew this was his way of asking about her year.

"A little, not too much. Dad has a tour coming up, you know. He's real busy."

Grandpa grunted and eased the car out onto the road. "And your mother?"

"She's busy, too, but not on tour this time. She's work-ing on some new pieces. And growing tomatoes, but they're pretty scraggly."

Grandpa laughed. "Your ma never did have a green thumb—she has a musical thumb! And what do you have, Maddy?"

Maddy looked out the window at the trees speeding by. It soothed her, to see that calm color and the wide blue sky. She chewed on her lip and shook her head. "I'm not sure what kind of thumb I have. They'd *like* me to be musical, but I'm just not. I don't know!" She shrugged her shoulders, unwilling to admit even to Grandpa how that worried her.

Grandpa turned off the highway and slowed on the narrow road. "Well, Sabrina and I have been waiting for you. We will pick raspberries and make jam that will make our lips and teeth red."

"Mmmm!"

"And there's lettuce and beans in the garden and some-thing leafy I don't know the name of."

"But I thought you knew the names of *everything*, Grandpa."

"Most things, pumpkin, not *all* things."

Maddy paused to let that sink in; that there were pieces of the world that went unnamed by Grandpa's firm voice, like dark corners of a room never touched by light.

"Has Sabrina been catching mice and birds? And leaving them on the floor like last year?"

"Mmm, last week she caught a warbler. Most distressing. Feathers all over the kitchen. I had to crawl around and pick them up with a wet paper towel. I scolded her, but you know it's her nature. Cats just like blood."

"Uck! Maybe that's why Mother would never let me get a cat."

"Nope, she really *is* allergic to cats. They make her break out in hives and sneeze eight times in a row. I've seen it happen."

Maddy leaned forward. They were going up the hill to Grandpa's house. She could almost see it. One more curve and it would be there, in front of her.

Grandpa turned into the drive, and the house shone yellow in the late summer sun. The shutters and door were a soft moss green. Sunflowers grew near the kitchen door, and a birdbath shimmered in the sunlight. And waiting on the step, round and black as velvet, was Sabrina.

In a second, Maddy was out of the car and sitting beside her cat. She put her nose into the cat's fur and took a deep sniff. Sweet, like a meadow or baking bread. A crow called once, its dark shadow winging over Maddy. Grandpa whistled a Scottish tune. Maddy took a deep breath and sighed. She was home.

CHAPTER THREE

They sat at the oak table in the kitchen, eating raspberries out of a blue bowl. Grandpa's lips were red. Maddy's mouth was red. Sabrina crouched under the table, nibbling on stray berries.

" 'Tain't natural," Grandpa complained. "The only cat I know of that likes raspberries."

"But she's not your ordinary cat," said Maddy, leaning down to rub Sabrina's head.

"That she's not," Grandpa said with his mouth full. "Now, I've got something different for you to see, Maddy."

He waved his arm toward a big black notebook on the kitchen counter. "I've been collecting stories all this spring, stories about these hills and valleys. I'll tell some of them to you when you're ready."

Maddy smiled at him. "OK, Grandpa. And don't forget we have to watch stars at night, the way we always do."

Grandpa nodded and repeated, "The way we always do."

For supper they had a whole bowl of beans from the garden and some pieces of wheat bread. That's what she loved about Grandpa; he didn't fuss. If he wanted to call a bowl of vegetables supper, he would do it. That would never happen with her parents. And when night came, Maddy slept in her own high, four-poster bed with Sabrina purring by her ear. Maddy could feel all the jagged pieces of the year settling down like bristly fur smoothed by a brush.

The next day Maddy wheeled her old green Raleigh bike out of the shed. Grandpa had already taken out his faulty ten-speed; only three of the gears worked. He was dressed in a wrinkled blue work shirt and khakis with bicycle clips on the bottom.

"You look like a Russian revolutionary," Maddy teased, swinging her leg over her bike. They'd studied a little of the Russian Revolution in school that year, and the pictures of the workers reminded her of Grandpa.

"I *am* a Russian revolutionary," Grandpa said, sitting

very upright on his bike. "I used to organize labor unions, remember?" He smoothed his big mustache proudly. "That was in the days when unions meant something."

"I know, I know," Maddy said, "and the police chased after you." She pushed off with her foot.

"Good thing they didn't catch me!" Grandpa yelled, leaning over his handlebars.

They sped down the steep hill to the church with the golden steeple, across the bridge, and along the road to the ice-cream stand. After they parked their bikes and got their cones, Grandpa took Maddy's arm and led her up the dirt road that went into the woods.

"Look at that." He swept his hand, as if giving her a present.

Maddy looked. It was the same as any summer country road: dusty brown, bordered by thick clumps of daisies and purple vetch and then merging into shadowy woods. A blue dragonfly buzzed low over them, making Maddy duck.

"I know they don't hurt you, Grandpa, but I can't help it. They're so big!"

Grandpa patted her arm. "Let me tell you about this road. I just learned a wonderful story last week. This isn't just *any* old road, Maddy. Things happen here, have happened here, and will happen again."

Maddy leaned close to him, taking in the smell of clean sweat and summer dust.

"At the end of this road is a hill and the remains of a house foundation. Long ago a pair of lovers fled down this road. The young woman stole the family's mare and cart, packed all her goods, including the butter churn and spinning wheel, and met her lover. You see, her family had forbidden the match. He was an undistinguished man with a thin mustache, but he was her own true love." Grandpa patted his thick mustache. "They raced along the road faster and faster, hitting the final curve on only two wheels—at least, that's what I've guessed. First the butter churn flew out of the wagon, then the spinning wheel. Her true love was hurled out of the wagon and killed when he hit a tree." Grandpa paused and took a breath. Maddy tightened her hand on his. "Then only the plunging horses and terrified woman were left."

"What did she do? Did she live?"

"I don't know. The horses galloped away with her, and she was never heard from again. But I do know this—she surely lived when she was racing down this road!"

"What does that mean? Wasn't she scared to death?"

"Maybe she liked it," Grandpa said, ruffling Maddy's hair. "Maybe she felt so alive she thought even death would be worth it to feel this singing in her veins."

This singing in her veins. What did that mean? All Maddy knew was that the road curved out of sight into shadows, with mystery strung along it like beads on a string. Would she be brave like that woman in the speeding wagon, daring anything? Maddy lifted her head at the faraway sound of a car horn, then turned to Grandpa.

"Let's see if we can find something that fell out of her wagon." Maddy started forward, excitement racing through her like a sudden flush of red. Maybe she could find a piece from the spinning wheel in the woods, if she only looked hard enough. Then it would be something all her own to take back and keep.

"Let's try the stream where the road curves, Maddy." Grandpa began to lope ahead of her, and she followed. They stopped at a narrow bridge over tumbling golden water. Grandpa scrambled down the bank and began to poke around near the rocks. "Maybe some spokes from the spinning wheel are in here, Maddy."

She was just about to leap over the bank when she heard a call, a high, fluting note that tugged at her. It felt like moonlight inside, white and silvery, and then it changed to a molten color, warm as an early sun.

Suddenly, a cat raced toward her, tail bristling. It was an immense tom, with a bitten ear and scarred nose. Maddy stepped back as the animal careened across the bridge. On its face it wore a fierce, triumphant expression, and on its back it wore a saddle.

CHAPTER FOUR

Nata spat into the grass. That tomcat! To run off in the middle of a hunt. What had gone wrong? Where he spat, a larkspur grew, tall and purple. Nata was so angry he could fly. He'd heard that anger could do that, lift you into the air. He was the only elf that would ever happen to, because he was the only elf he knew who got truly angry. But the worst of it was the loss of his saddle, the one Hele had made for him. Covered in deerskin, dyed green and decorated with red whorls and stars, it was the most beautiful saddle he'd ever had. And it signaled her intent to marry him.

Cala, his cousin, turned on the shoulders of his tomcat and shrugged. He whispered, "A pity, that fine mount!"

Nata tightened his mouth and held his arrow ready against the string of his long, curved bow. Cats were meant to obey elves, but sometimes one came along who did not. A large blue dragonfly had crazed Nata's mount, sending him leaping and skittering until Nata fell off, and the cat raced away.

Nata kept his eyes fixed on the entrance to the rabbit's burrow. His neck prickled as a fierce cry tore through the air. Then his shoulders eased down; it was a hawk, not an owl. He remembered the warning Sala had given just this morning.

"The Horned One is about," Sala had said. "I heard his scream in the forest last night. Be careful where you go, and don't go far."

But there were no rabbits near camp; all had been hunted or lost to some mysterious disease. They *had* to have meat. Nata shivered. Maybe The Horned One had marked him out. Hadn't the owl devoured Nata's parents years ago, when Nata was just a child? Maybe He had a taste for their blood.

Nata tried to concentrate on the rabbit. He could feel the scrabbles of the buck's paws on dirt, the strong, powerful thrusts of his back legs against the tunnel walls.

The grasses moved by the burrow's entrance. *Now!* The buck's paws dug into the earth; a nose appeared at the entrance. Cautiously, the rabbit thrust his head out into the light and stayed still for minutes. Nata waited as the wind whispered of a turquoise sea and the clouds sang of high mountains.

The buck eased through the grasses by the burrow. He stiffened and sniffed the air. Nata and Cala were downwind, so the rabbit could not catch their scent. His nose twitched. Nata could feel the whiskers testing the air, taking in the heat of the grass, the smells on the breeze. Nata did not breathe.

Slowly the buck eased forward, striped by the brown shade of the grass. Nata's bowstring twanged, the buck leapt, screamed, and fell to the ground. Cala jumped off his mount and rushed forward. Because Nata was the elder, he would slit the buck's throat and make sure all the dangerous blood ran into the dry summer earth.

Once the stinging blood was safely gone into the soil, Cala skinned the rabbit with swift, sure strokes. The women would take the skin, scrape it and stretch it on a frame, knead it with oils and herbs, and use it for bedding and clothing. Together, the two elves carved the rabbit into smaller pieces and packed them into grass-net carrying bags. The lining of birch leaves would keep blood from dripping onto their shoulders, for blood burned where it touched elf skin.

Nata rolled the rabbit's pelt in a hunting cloth, shifted it onto his shoulders, and took up a sack filled with meat. The other bag was already tied to the high back of Cala's saddle. The cat stepped into shadow, and they set off for home.

With Cala riding slowly, Nata followed on foot, glancing at the sky from time to time. Although owls hunted at night, The Horned One did not obey the laws of owls or elves. He hunted when He pleased, whom He pleased.

Cala looked over his shoulder. "We will have to get up a hunting party to rid the woods of this menace," he said.

"And I'll be first in line to shoot Him!" Nata said. He stalked behind his cousin, still angry at the loss of his tom. How foolish he'd look coming back to camp on foot. He tried to calm his anger before they neared camp, knowing how it upset the other elves. Anger was hated almost as much as blood. Nata wished he were more like his companions: calm, never interested in those strange creatures called humans.

A sudden melancholy descended upon him like a suffocating cloud. It happened sometimes to elves, he knew, but never before to him. The air darkened. The leaves did not rustle, singing their silver songs. The moss did not spring up under his feet, bringing news of icy streams deep underground.

He stopped, watching Cala disappear into the glade

where their camp was hidden. Was it worry about The Horned One that darkened the air, muting the calls of the world? He knelt to pick a partridgeberry and munched on it. The sweet red taste flowed down his throat, and he felt better. Standing, he listened to a wren crying:

Blue jay, open mouth,
ate my brood,
swallowed them down.
Woe is me!

He sent an orange note to the wren, who scooped it up in her beak and gulped it down. Immediately, her song changed and became sweeter, more hopeful.

Suddenly, the songs of the world burst up through the forest floor: the shrill cries of hunting shrews, the crackling calls of insects, the slow wanderings of roots nudging through soil. Nata took a deep, calming breath. Could he not sing plants up out of the earth in the spring? Did he not call to the great snow geese in the fall until they released their feathers to drift at his feet, making a blanket fit for a king?

Only elves can do such things! thought Nata, clenching his fists. They would find a way to vanquish this new threat. He began to sing as he went forward to greet the others. And as he sang, new grass sprang up behind him.

CHAPTER FIVE

While Cala took the cat to the barns, Nata stood on the edge of camp. Then he knelt by the nearby stream and washed the last of the blood off the rabbit meat until the water ran clear. He wrapped it again in fresh grass and hoisted it onto his back. Talk wafted toward him as the camp of thirty elves and ten youngsters sat close together under the setting sun.

"Maybe we should leave some meat out for Him. He could eat it and let us alone," said Nala, a stripling.

Sala rubbed his chin. "It would have to be live meat, Nala, and I don't think it would work. It is not meat He wants but elves! You remember how He took Nata's mother and father years back."

The words floated across camp to Nata. He was not ready to be part of the talk just yet. Sucking in a breath, he remembered how the great, hooked claws of the owl had seized his mother, lifting her into the air. How his father had tried to stab The Horned One's belly, but the thick covering of feathers defeated him. How the very next night, as the elves searched for the owl, Nata's father had also been snatched and borne off into the dark sky, never to be seen again.

Uneasy, children rustled and leaned against their parents. They sensed something was wrong, but were too little to understand it.

"We will have to start going out in groups of three or four, always armed. When you work in the gardens, bring your bows and arrows. When you go for water, never go without your weapons." Sala plucked a leaf and tore it to shreds. His face wore a wearied, sad look.

The elves nodded in agreement, and someone hummed a fragment of song. They had noticed the young ones beginning to twitter with fear, their faces paling silver in the late afternoon light.

But another stripling began to talk of owls again. "I still

do not understand why the owls don't obey us," he said. "All the other creatures of the wood, the water, and the air do."

"Hush," said an elder, "you've heard the tale before."

Nata listened and shivered; this story always reminded him that everything could have been different. If only.

"It is well to remember again," Sala said as he sipped from a bowl of birch tea. "Long ago, just after we came to this country of forests, an elf violated the covenant with owls. You remember what the covenant says: 'You may eat of the animals of the field—voles, weasels, rabbits, mice, moles—and any of the fishes of the streams and sea. But the birds of the air, you may not kill. They belong to the wind and cannot be hunted by you.'"

Sala paused and sipped again. "But one wild, fiery elf decided he must have a special cape for courting his true love. He shot an arrow at an owl winging home one morning. The arrow pierced the bird, who fell screaming to the ground. None of the other elves dared touch the dead owl. But that foolish elf plucked all the feathers to make his courting cape. The other owls heard of this, and from that time on, owls do not listen to elves."

"In spite of our offerings of plump moles on the forest floor," said Nala.

For a moment, they all sat with their heads bowed under the weight of that long-ago deed. Nata shivered and stepped forward into a slant of light. He was tired of being on the outside; he wanted to sit next to Hele and sip birch tea with the rest of the camp.

"Nata!" Hele left the circle to run forward and greet him. "You're back!" She did not say any more, but the pressure of her fingers on his arm told him she had been worried.

He took the cup of birch tea she offered and swung his meat down at her feet. She smiled, saying, "This is welcome, indeed. I thought all we would have for supper was *risele*."

The other elves murmured and smiled at them, happy to think of something more cheerful than the owl. Hele put the fresh meat into a clay pot suspended over the fire. Into it she threw rosemary, bay, carrots, and the lacy purple leaves of *risele*. Soon the sweet scent of cooking meat circled through the camp, and the elves began to talk eagerly of past hunts and past glories.

"Thank you," said Sala. "We have been hungry for meat."

"What did you see, Nata?" Lele asked, taking out her ashwood harp. "Any tales I can weave into a song?"

Nata rubbed his chin ruefully. He was not ready to tell of losing his mount, though Sala would have to know.

"We saw tall grass, a wren who lost her brood, and heard clouds talking of cold skies," sang Nata in a low voice.

Cala took up the chant. "And the shadows waved over

us as we waited for the buck, listening to the thump of his paws inside his burrow."

"We waited, listening," Nata went on, and Lele strummed a chord. "We waited as the clouds chattered among themselves. Then the rabbit thrust his head out, tested the air . . ." He paused politely, giving his cousin a chance to continue.

"And we let loose our arrows, which dove into his fur and took his life away."

The group sighed, and the notes rose over them. Lele sang in a high, sweet voice of past hunts, of rabbits who had lived for years before being caught by them, and of the threads that bound them to all living things.

After the song and stories were ended, Hele took the rabbit out of the pot and carved it into pieces, a small bite for everyone. The little ones did not eat meat; their bodies were not yet strong enough for it. They would sup on the vegetables and broth.

Suddenly, Nata had to tell what had happened to his mount. He felt wrapped in shame, sitting in the light of their warm regard, with no one but Cala knowing about the lost cat. He *had* to tell them; keeping this secret felt almost as terrible as mouthing a lie.

"Sala," he began slowly.

Sala raised his head. "And what do you have to tell us, Nata?" He smiled kindly at him.

"My mount ran away from me and would not heed my

call." Nata spread his hands, ashamed. "Do you think there is something wrong that he would not listen to me?"

Sala laughed, a rich, earthy sound. "Wrong? In a cat disobeying an elf? It has happened before, young one, it has happened before! Though"—he paused and pulled on one long ear—"it *should* have listened to you. You know all the calls to make animals come when wanted, leave when wanted, run when wanted. And our mounts eat *tileen,* berries that make them more obedient. Why do you think your tom ran away?"

Nata looked at his cousin and shrugged his shoulders. "He was tempted by a great blue dragonfly, but . . . What do you think?"

Cala shifted uncomfortably on the ground. "Maybe we were too near the road, Nata. I wondered at the time. We were close enough so I could hear a car horn."

Sala frowned. "You know better. In silence is safety, in deep woods is calm." He repeated the ancient litany. "Still, we must not live so far from humans that we cannot get our mounts."

"I know, Sala, I know," Nata muttered. But the worst of it was, the cat had his saddle on, the gift from Hele. Nata could hardly bear to speak the words before the other elves. To lose such a valuable thing! Why had he not ridden barebacked?

But Sala anticipated him. "Did your mount wear a saddle this day?"

"Yes, he did." Nata hung his head.

"Then we must get the cat back at once, before some greedy human finds him and comes to search for us here in our safe woods. That saddle will look like nothing they have ever seen. You know what the rule is about losing a mount wearing a saddle and bridle, Nata!"

"Couldn't they just think the tack is something for a house pet or a toy?" Hele asked, her hand close to Nata's.

"People *are* stupid, most of them, but from time to time a human comes along who has eyes that can see. What if he or she really *sees* that saddle on the cat?"

"All right, I know what must be done." Nata rose wearily, hoisting his bow and arrows over his shoulders. "I will set off at once to look for the cat." How could he have been so stupid to let it go? He should have left the hunting to Cala and run off immediately to get his mount back. But he had forgotten the rule. He had been too busy trying to get meat for the camp and worrying about The Horned One.

When he turned to go, Hatele and Nala rose and followed. "You must not go alone, Nata, it is too dangerous. We will come, too, and call on the moonlight to light our way."

As they spoke, the last of the sun's rays vanished behind the tall pines. Lele strummed on her harp again and began a ballad of elves in the old green country. No one could guess in that soft time of song that the owl and the lost saddle were the beginning of the end of their life in that forest.

Chapter Six

Finally, she was alone! Maddy threw off her clothes, pulled on her nightgown, and jumped onto the bed. Always before, she'd stay with Grandpa until the very last moment before bed, drawing out their time together. "One more game of Monopoly, Grandpa? How about another story?" Anything to keep them knitted together.

But on this night, Maddy had gone to bed early, racing up the stairs as Grandpa called after her, "One more game of Monopoly, pumpkin? How about another story?" For she had to think about that cat, the one she'd seen earlier, running away with a saddle on its back.

Maddy lay against the pillows. How did she know he was running away? Pulling on her bottom lip, she thought back—remembering the road and the cat. Stones shining in the light. Puffs of dust floating in the sunlight by the bridge. The sudden, bursting sight of the scarred face and triumphant look in the animal's eyes. It was the look she'd sometimes seen when Sabrina escaped outside—a wide-eyed, victorious expression.

Maddy began to hum to herself; it helped her think. On the cat was a green saddle, high in the front and back, with red designs along the edges. And there was a bridle on his face, too. A beautifully fitted, polished bridle. She squinted her eyes, as if that would help her to see better. No shine on the saddle, as sunlight would gleam on plastic. Leather, it had to be leather, and beautifully made. *Someone* had spent a very great deal of time working on that tack, dying the leather, inscribing the designs. "Not a toy," Maddy whispered, "definitely *not* a toy."

If anyone had asked her why, she might have thought, rubbing her lip and then replying, "Too expensive. And besides, there was the rope."

The rope! Maddy sat up in bed, hugging her knees. Now she remembered; there had been a small coil of rope hung over the pommel. For what? Roping tiny steers? Maddy did not laugh, puzzling it out instead. To tie up the cat, like a leash? But you could tie him with the reins.

But *who* used the rope and for *what*? As Maddy's thoughts skittered away, part of her mind kept working on the puzzle. Holding her hand upright, Maddy judged the height of the cat at the shoulder to be five inches. Five inches! Anything that could ride a cat and not drag its feet upon the ground would have to be—Maddy held the other hand up on top of the first, and counted—about eight or nine inches. "Sitting," Maddy said to herself, and Sabrina nudged her.

Sitting! Who was sitting on the cat; *what* was sitting on him? Then suddenly, all the thoughts that had buzzed and circled about inside dove through her head and disappeared. She did not call them back. She did not want an answer to this mystery—not just yet. Maddy hummed to herself, taking courage from the everydayness of her room. But this would be *her* mystery, something special belonging only to her. *Like the magic moments framed in silver in the living room at home,* thought Maddy.

She ran her fingers along the edge of the patchwork quilt. It had a soft, worn feel that never failed to comfort her. This had been Grandma's quilt, made by her, with golden appliquéd sunflowers nodding over strips of green calico grass. Sometimes in the night, Maddy would wake up and see the sunflowers glowing in the moonlight, like a magic garden she could enter all on her own.

Magic. That burst of air, that rush of sound as the cat came silently around the corner. *How can something quiet be noisy?* Maddy thought. But he had been so. Something in the force and speed of the cat, propelling it forward, had blown toward her like a cyclone's wind. She'd had to step back from the road into the trees; lucky Grandpa didn't see, fishing for things in the stream under the bridge.

But will it be wonderful? Maddy wondered, hugging her legs tightly. *This magic?* Books spoke of magic as if it were a kind of sweet spice in an autumn pie—something to savor and delight in—something almost cozy. That wild, scarred cat in a rush of noise and speed had nothing cozy about him. He bespoke danger, wildness, and something fierce and deep like a drumbeat under faraway music—barely heard, but definitely there.

Maddy lay down and pulled the covers up to her chin, reaching out to touch Sabrina. Her fur was soft and warm, comforting. Back home Mother and Daddy would be reading in their living room, listening to music. Did they miss her? Right now they seemed distant to Maddy, like people on another planet. That fierce, escaping cat had sucked her into something so different, so puzzling, that Maddy knew she would not even miss home until she unraveled or solved this mystery.

CHAPTER SEVEN

Nata pushed wearily through the underbrush. He had been looking for that tom for hours now, his two companions beside him. Nala seemed to think it was his personal responsibility to guard Nata's back; he kept his bow strung, ready to loose an arrow should he hear the owl's hunting cry. Hatele crouched by his side, her ears swiveling on their stalks with each new sound.

Stopping for a moment, Nala checked the trail they'd been following. He wiped his brow. "I think that cat has headed for the country of humans."

"Mother of the forest! Don't say that! If he's gone to humans, we *are* in trouble." Nata thumped his fist against his side. "All these years, what has Sala dinned into us? That no cat must ever be lost with its tack on."

He pulled his cap lower. "I think my wits were wandering today or . . ." His voice trailed off.

"We *all* are afraid of The Horned One," Hatele put in. "He is enough to make any rule fly out of our heads!"

Nata touched her shoulder gratefully and sighed. "But still I wonder why that cat disobeyed me."

"That's a cat for you," Hatele said, shifting her bow and arrows against her back.

Nata moved under the low branch of a birch tree; the shelter made his heart beat more slowly. Now the moon was waning in the sky; soon it would be dawn. No sign of his cat, no sign of the saddle. And luckily, no sign of The Horned One. But what could he tell Sala? How would the wise one ever trust him again? Pursing his lips, Nata kept on, hoping he would find something before dawn came, taking comfort from the nearness of his companions.

When the moon had finally sunk out of sight and the sun was cresting over the horizon, the elves straggled back to camp to lie on deerskins spread over pine needles. Just as Nata was falling asleep, Maddy was stretching awake in her bed.

"Ah!" she sighed, swinging her legs out of the covers.

Sabrina chirruped to her and leapt onto the floor. One of the things Maddy loved about Grandpa's house was the way the sun came in her window in the morning. The light lay in wide beams across the floor, as if it were a carpet she could step on. Birds chattered in the branches outside her window, and one branch tapped comfortingly against the pane when the wind blew. She felt surrounded by friends and warmth.

"Grandpa?" She ran downstairs with Sabrina at her heels. "Are you up?"

" 'Course I'm up, lazybones. It's all of seven-thirty, you know. I've been up for an hour at least, talking to the blue jays, waiting for you to roll out of bed."

"Pooh!" She blew him a kiss and got herself some breakfast: granola from the tall brown cupboard and milk from the fridge. She sat beside him.

"What are we going to do today, Grandpa? Go exploring? I'd like to go back to that ice-cream stand." She did not say that she would be looking for a cat with a saddle on. Maybe she would tell Grandpa about it another day.

"I don't know about you, but we've got a problem right at our door, Maddy." He rose and pointed outside. "See that cat? He's been sitting there all morning—all night, as far as I know! And he shows no sign of leaving."

Maddy rose and looked through the window. She gasped. It was the wide-faced tom she'd seen yesterday running down the dirt road. Except now, his back was bare.

"What? What is it? I felt your shoulders hunch up. You've seen this cat before, Maddy?"

Shaking her head, Maddy felt gooseflesh prickling her arms. Why was that animal sitting and staring at their house? "Is Sabrina in heat, Grandpa?"

"Nope, I had her fixed years ago. You know that. Are you holding out on me, Maddy? You know something."

"No, no." Sabrina rubbed against Maddy's legs, purring, and Maddy gave her an absentminded pat. "I thought maybe I saw that cat when we were on the dirt road—the one where the woman escaped with her lover."

"Oh." He seemed satisfied and went back to sip the rest of his coffee at the table. "Maybe he followed us home."

"Running after the car, Grandpa?" Maddy turned and took her dishes over to the sink.

"Sure, cats do that sometimes. Didn't you see *Homeward Bound*?"

"Yes, I saw it. I'm going out for a bit, Grandpa, on my own, please. I need to . . . to think about this tomcat," she finished, standing in the doorway.

Grandpa grinned at her. "OK, pumpkin."

Feeling vaguely guilty, Maddy crept down the steps and stood ten feet away from the sitting tom. She looked at him, and he stared back. The same wide face, the same bitten ear, the same sleek, well-cared-for body.

Chirruping, she walked around him. "Here, kitty, here kitty." But he did not respond.

Sabrina followed, stepping carefully up to the other animal. They touched noses as Sabrina swished her tail slowly, back and forth.

"All right, all right, be friends, you two!" Maddy admonished them. Sabrina gave a stange chirp and sniffed the tom thoroughly from head to toe. He sat there, impassive and silent. Wasn't the tom supposed to sniff Sabrina, too? It seemed as if he were drenched in some strange, enticing scent that only Sabrina could smell. The two cats began to purr in unison, and Maddy laughed.

"Friends at last!" *But where's the saddle?* Leaving the cats, Maddy walked down Grandpa's driveway. She found an old stick and began to swish it at the grass, back and forth. Nothing by the drive. Across the field she went methodically; down the left side, up the middle, down the right, parting the grass each step of the way. She began to think she would never find it. After all, the cat could have bitten through the belly strap in the woods where she first saw him. Or the saddle could be lost in the forest somewhere. But somehow, Maddy could not stop looking; she could *see* that saddle so clearly that she just knew it wasn't lost.

After searching for a good half hour, Maddy came to

stop under one of Grandpa's ancient apple trees. The gnarled and twisted tree lay on flattened grass. Once, when the tree was still upright, a wood duck had nested in the trunk. Maddy remembered the bright, dark eye of the duck as it stared up at her from the tree cavity. Maddy stooped and poked her stick under the fallen trunk. Her stick caught on something green. Lichen? Moss? She reached in carefully and closed her fingers on something firm and shaped.

Drawing her hand out of the shadows, Maddy saw she was holding a leather saddle about three inches wide by four inches long—green, with red whorls scribing its sides. The back was high and solid to keep its rider safely on the mount. On the front of the saddle was a small pommel with the rope still tied to it. It was all strangely familiar, yet infinitely exotic and strange. She lifted the saddle to her nose and breathed in. A wild, minty, sharp scent rose, and suddenly the air seemed blue, charged with green specks. A faint song belled, and Maddy dropped the saddle.

A shiver started deep inside her, working its way up her body until she had to cry out. This was not play; this was not a child's toy. This was the working saddle of someone very small who rode cats.

CHAPTER EIGHT

"There is nothing to be done, then," Sala said, letting his hands fall to his side. He stood in front of Nata at the morning council, where the tasks of the day were decided. "Your mount is gone—with his tack—and cannot be found."

Nata hung his head miserably. "We did try, wise one; we looked through the forest."

Sala put his hand on Nata's shoulder. "I am reluctant to punish you, Nata, and think that your worry over The

Horned One made you careless—you who have lost so much to that owl."

Nata nodded. "But it must *never* happen again. Remember—we can only live so close to humans if we are careful—always." Sala paused, wrinkling his brow. "Let us hope that cat bit through his belly strap and left the saddle lying in the forest. They will do that, and scrape the bridle off against a tree. Then no human will find it and try to solve the mystery of that saddle and bridle."

Nata pulled on his hair, and silver sparks spun up into the air. He heard Hele sighing behind him. She was relieved, he knew. Nata also knew that Sala was being kind—this time.

"Now off with you! You must replace your lost mount right away, for we need every hunter we have to protect the camp from The Horned One."

Happy to get away, Nata headed toward the road to find a new cat. In the bag slung over his shoulder were two moles he'd just caught. It took him some time to make his way through the forest to the place where the trees thinned. Finally, he lowered himself to the ground, opened his mouth, and called. The song curled up in a whorl of green notes. Nata watched the small globes sail off over the trees. Just to be sure, he sucked in a breath and again blew out the sounds that would pluck at a cat's heart and make it run away from humans, through the woods to him.

He twitched the bag, impatient and excited. Who

would come leaping into the sunlight this time? The waiting, the wondering was the best part in calling a new mount. Would it be black with white patches? Would it be mottled orange and brown with a good-tempered nose and green eyes? This new mount must be better than his last, who was bad-tempered, even before he ran off after that blue dragonfly.

It would be easier, of course, if they could breed their own cats. They had tried it, but it had not been a success. Maybe the berries they gave their mounts to make them more obedient interfered with breeding. Still, it was the excitement of calling cats that Nata loved. He was glad they could not breed their own.

He watched the clouds overhead. "Fine weather," they called out in the thin, prickly voice of ice. "Sun, blue skies, clean, crisp air."

Nata smiled. Good weather to catch a cat in, not the wrong kind of weather, which was hot and wet, making the cats sharp clawed and uneasy. Nata tapped his foot. An animal should be coming soon. He opened the top of his carrying bag. Next to the two moles was a bunch of the minty green leaves that cats loved, that made them roll over and wave their paws in the air, grinning foolishly.

There. A soft step on leaves beyond the glade. Nata peered into the shadows. A chipmunk scolded and scurried out of sight. A chickadee flew overhead, calling, "Not my brood, evil one, not my brood today!" She dashed down over something unseen, chittering and fluttering her wings.

The cat entered the glade and stopped, eyeing Nata. Black fur shone in the light, and its eyes glowed green.

"Come," sang Nata, holding out his hand. "I will feed you and care for you; I will keep all dogs at bay. Come."

The cat crept forward, belly scraping moss. Step by step, it inched toward the elf and then lay in front of him, chin on outstretched paws. Nata crouched beside it and caressed its nose. He blew softly into its nostrils, and the cat quivered with delight. Slowly Nata went around the animal, touching here, probing there. Some scars on the right flank, where the hair grew thin, probably from a long-ago fight. A lovely paintbrush end to its tail, a sign of good temper. This one was a female, and Nata preferred toms, but she was high in the leg and broad in the shoulder—perfect for hunting.

He knelt and sniffed her fur. Humans. She was a house cat, not a barn or a meadow cat. His nose wrinkled. He smelled strange food, the warmth of blankets, and a special scent that made him visualize a small human face with gray eyes. Never before had he had a vision of a human face. It tantalized him. If only he could see this person—just once!

Nata sat back on his heels, keeping his hand on the cat. It was against all laws to be seen by a human, but he wished he could know just *one.* Although they were gigantic, humans did not look all *that* different from elves, or so he had heard. Nata sighed. The old ones always said that banishment was the punishment for being seen by a human, but Nata had never actually heard of it happening.

"Humans are dangerous," Sala said, "always ready to use an elf for evil purposes."

But did Sala tell all the truth? What of the old days when elf families and human families had been linked, or so the ancient tales went? Nata resolved then and there to go see old Ela in the House of Scrolls. He would ask Ela questions; he would read the scrolls to see what they said of humans.

Nata drew a mole out of his bag, setting it before the cat, who sniffed it, then began to chew eagerly. As her rumblings filled the air, Nata drew a leather cord around the animal's neck to hold her fast. While she ate, Nata sang softly:

> *You will have long naps in the warm sun,*
> *brushings to make your fur tingle,*
> *wild hunts through the forest,*
> *and a long and full life.*

Nata knew the elves' cats—like all cats—would finally die, but they would have longer-than-normal lives in elfin company.

When the mole was eaten, the cat was his. He led her by the cord back to camp. Running his hand lightly over the cat's head, Nata took her to a moss bed at the end of a high, walled pen. She twitched her nose at the scent of the other animals but lay obediently on the moss. Only after he had seen her safely settled in did Nata leave for the House of Scrolls, knowing everyone else would be busy in the camp at this hour. If he were ever to find out about humans, this would be the time.

CHAPTER NINE

Nata went to the birch lodge at the far end of the clearing. It was reserved for ceremonies and storing the scrolls that recorded their long history, songs, story cycles, and laws.

Pulling aside the skin door, he walked in. Ela, the keeper of the scrolls, was dozing in a wooden chair, feet propped on another chair.

"Mmmmph?" He started as Nata went behind him to the tightly woven baskets where the scrolls were stored.

"You here, young one?" He pushed his moleskin cap

back and peered at Nata. "What do you want with the scrolls, eh? Do you want to see the songs for the Binding Ceremony? I hear you and Hele . . ." He paused, grinning.

Nata tried to smile. "Not yet, not yet, Ela. You know we are too young. I have not reached seventy-five years."

He wondered how old Ela was. Ela moved more slowly now, and the lines on his face seemed filled with dust. His ears had broadened and flattened to his head over the centuries. Would Ela leave his body soon? Only once had Nata seen that happen, when an elf, after five hundred years of life, had finally left his body. And he had never forgotten how frightening was that final mystery.

Ela interrupted Nata's thoughts by sneezing abruptly, three times in a row. "Usually it's the old ones or visiting elves who want to read the scrolls. What are you looking for?" He stood and stretched, pulling his cap off and giving his sparse hair a good rub.

"I want to see the scrolls about humans, Ela. I know we're not meant to think about them, but they don't live so far away, and they've been on my mind lately."

"Not good to have humans on the mind, young one." Ela shook his finger at Nata. He went to a near basket, grunting as he pulled off the tight-fitting lid. He took out two scrolls and set them on a low table.

Nata sat down. "I just want to see what the scrolls say about people. I already know what Sala says."

"Impatient, full of passion, greedy, cruel, intemperate,

can never stick to one thing for long." Ela ticked off the characteristics on one hand. "Of course, when you only live for seventy-five years, it's probably *hard* to stick to one thing for long."

Nata untied the thong that bound the first scroll. Unrolling it, he smelled lavender and dried fall leaves. Runes burned into the bark flowed and coiled like tree roots across the page. Small flowers and stars were interwoven in their designs, outlined in green and brown. Nata read the top lines.

"This is the first scroll to mention humans. It is not agreed among us how much should be known about them, the *laglan*. Remember that *laglan* also refers to something sharp, explosive, and dangerous. Some elves believe the less known the better. Others, myself among them, believe we must know our enemy. Although we were not always enemies, as you shall see."

Silently, Nata read on. "A long time ago in the green country, when only elves and unicorns leapt over the grass, there was no disharmony, no evil. All spoke in the tongue of elves, and long did the sweetness last. Then men came. At first we befriended them, showing them the best herbs for healing, the best for cooking, and where the magic mushrooms grew in rings. Sometimes an elf family linked themselves to a human family, in a partnership that lasted many generations. But then humans became greedy. They demanded that we cure their illnesses and keep them from growing old. They saw that elves stayed bounding and young while they withered and decayed.

"Over the centuries we retreated into the hills and became only a legend to them, never letting them see us except for a few chosen souls. I, alone, believe that there are still a few special humans left like our friends from long ago.

"But this is what is said of the *laglan*: greedy, quick to anger, slow to forgive. A long memory for vengeance, a short one for love. They think they are the only living beings with a right to life. They cannot hear the songs of the world, the whisperings of water, the speech of ferns. That may explain the deep sadness we sometimes see in humans. Therefore, ever shall our ways be separate, to preserve the life of elves and our life as caretakers of nature. Here ends the first scroll of humans, signed, Mila, the scholar."

Nata pushed back his chair and stood, rolling up the scroll. It was as bad as Sala said . . . and yet? He rubbed his face and sighed. At one time humans and elves had been friends, even joined in a kind of partnership. Suddenly, he wished *he* could be linked to that small, pointed face with the gray eyes, the one he had visualized after smelling the new cat's fur.

Nata decided not to open the second scroll, having read all he wished to for now.

"Did you find what you wanted to know?" Ela asked, startling Nata. Nata handed the scrolls back to the elder.

"A little," he answered. "I was hoping to find that somehow we might still have links with a few humans in this land." Nata sighed and stretched, feeling a deep ache inside. "It is lonely sometimes, Ela."

"Lonely? *Lonely?*" Ela clapped his hat tighter onto his head. "How can you want more than the companionship of elves, Nata?"

"But there are so *few* of us." Nata rubbed his face wearily. The old one would never understand.

"Few because we daren't live together, young chuck! If it weren't for the murdering humans, we could live nearer the elves in the cold country, the elves of the desert, or the elves by the shining river. Then we could have the great summer feasts of old, with weeks of singing, eating, and telling tales." Ela sighed.

"I wish we could, too. Have *you* ever seen a human or talked with one?" Nata asked.

Ela pursed his lips. "Once, long ago, before the rule of banishment, I did try to speak with one in the deep woods. But his eyes and ears were closed to me. He could not see me or hear my words. I have never tried again. Listen to Sala; safety lies in silence, deep woods, and blind humans."

Nata wanted to say "But we live in the same world!" It was strange, but now that he had read the scroll, he wanted more than ever to see and speak with a human, even though he knew it meant danger.

Closing the door behind him, Nata walked slowly back to the lodge he shared with his cousins, wondering if he had gone mad.

CHAPTER TEN

Maddy lay with her eyes closed, thinking. Why had that tomcat come to their house? He had stayed near all yesterday, even after Maddy found the saddle. But at sundown, he had mysteriously disappeared into the forest. Sabrina gave a mournful cry, but did not follow.

Maddy turned over and flung her arm out, fingers searching for Sabrina. Touching a bare sheet, Maddy pulled her hand back and sat up. Sabrina! Where was she? There was no soft, inquiring nudge into her cheek, no rumbling purr beside her ear. Always Sabrina waited for Maddy to get up before she went downstairs to nose her water dish and food.

Maddy climbed out of the four-poster bed and pulled on her clothes. Before leaving her room, she knelt and peered under the bed. Lying in the shadows under her bed was the saddle, like some exotic creature washed up on a beach. Later. She would deal with that later, Maddy thought, running to the kitchen to look at Sabrina's dish. The mound of brown kibbles was barely touched; the water dish was to the brim as well.

Opening the door, Maddy went out on the stoop. Sunflowers leaned against the yellow clapboards of the house. She watched a bee plunge into a flower and hang there, grumbling to itself.

"Sabrina?" she called. "Sabrina? Here, kitty, kitty, kitty." Standing on tiptoe, Maddy peered out across the meadow. Gray light from the cloudy sky made it hard to see. There was no telltale parting of the grass, no chirrup of greeting from her cat. Had Sabrina gone off with that tom from yesterday? Maddy had an instant's terrible premonition of loss, as if the Pied Piper of Hamelin had called to her cat, and she had disappeared into the mountain, never to return.

Grandpa came out and sat on the top step. He touched her arm, saying, "Sit, pumpkin, it's too early to stand. What's wrong?"

"Sabrina's gone, Grandpa, and she's hardly eaten anything or drunk from her water dish. She always waits for me before she gets up."

"Maybe she's off on an adventure," Grandpa said, "like the Australian aborigines who go on a walkabout. Maybe she got tired of being a good kitty and went off to make trouble somewhere with that tom. She can go out whenever she wants." He pointed to the cat flap in the bottom of the kitchen door.

"Maybe," Maddy said, still looking out across the fields, "but I don't think she would do that, Grandpa. I just got here; she wouldn't go off and leave me!"

"She might if she had a boyfriend," said Grandpa, grinning.

"Pooh! Why does she need a boyfriend when she has me?" asked Maddy, worrying at a scab on her bare knee.

"Let's see if this will bring her back." Grandpa pulled a blade of grass from the patch beside the porch and cupped his hands around the blade. He blew hard, and a sharp wail flew out of his hands. "She'll come to scold me for being too noisy."

Maddy leaned against him, knowing he would feel her sadness, like a trickle of icy water. He would help.

Giving her a tight hug, Grandpa rose and said, "Don't imagine a disaster, honey, it's early days yet. She's probably off on a toot with that other cat and will be home by suppertime."

"I don't want to wait till suppertime, Grandpa! She could be hurt or lost or . . ." She swung her arms, cold with a sense of impending loss.

"This isn't like you, Maddy, to be such a worrier." Grandpa peered into her face. "What's up?"

Shaking her head, Maddy moved away from him. She couldn't tell Grandpa about the saddle on the tom; she couldn't tell him about the air turning blue and the faint song rising when she touched the saddle. That was *her* mystery—for now, at least.

Grandpa touched her arm gently. "Give her time to turn up, OK? Come work in the garden with me, and if she's not back by the afternoon, we'll go looking for her."

"I think I'll go look in the woods, Grandpa. You work in the garden. I just have this feeling. . . ." Her words trailed off as Maddy turned and went toward the dense growth of trees. He waved to her and walked down to his garden patch.

Though Maddy searched throughout the trees, down the path, out to the stream, and even to the ridge that overlooked the busy road below, there was no sign of either Sabrina or the wide-faced tomcat.

"I wonder if she could be near that ice-cream stand, Grandpa," Maddy said later in the day.

"Why do you think she's there? That's a ways for Sabrina to travel, Maddy."

"I don't know, Grandpa," said Maddy, not looking up from her sandwich. "I just have a feeling."

"OK, then let's get in the car and go." They drove through the fog and parked by the wet tables.

When they climbed out of the car, Maddy almost told Grandpa about the saddle. The words bunched behind her lips. But she just could not let them out, not yet. This was still *her* mystery, and she felt that Sabrina might be in the woods, maybe led here by that tom.

Fog dripped from the sun umbrellas. One sad-looking boy mouthed a cone while his mother chivied him. "Come on, Frank, come on! I haven't got all day, and besides, this isn't an ice-cream day."

The boy mumbled, "Every day is an ice-cream day," but his mother didn't hear, jiggling her foot and drumming her red-painted fingernails on the table.

Starting down the dirt road, Maddy motioned for Grandpa to follow.

"OK, OK, I'm coming, Maddy. I don't see why you think Sabrina's here—that tom was up by the house—but I'm a mild-mannered man, like Clark Kent." Grandpa loped beside her.

Maddy didn't smile, though she usually did at Grandpa's jokes. He knew all the comic books, all the cartoons on television. It was one of the things she loved in him, that he even got up early to watch *Conan the Adventurer.* Certainly, her parents would never do that.

"Here, kitty!" Maddy called as they walked over the bridge, her footsteps echoing hollowly. "Here, Sabrina, come here!"

Then Grandpa added his voice to hers. "Here, kitty, kitty, kitty. Although I do think the way to call a cat is like this, Maddy: pssst, pssst, pssst!"

Maddy hardly heard, peering through the undergrowth, searching for signs of Sabrina. Mist swirled about the tree trunks, now showing a patch of white birch, now showing a rain-soaked brown maple.

"Here, kitty," called Maddy. "Here, kitty!" For one quick, sharp moment, she knew what it would be to never see her cat again. Her chest felt hollow, and her fingers trembled. "Here, kitty, kitty."

Echoing and bouncing off the mist, Maddy's voice sounded strange even to her. She was sure her cat would never recognize that sound.

"Grandpa?" She tugged on his arm. "Could you wait here while I go into the woods? If she's on the road, then you'll see her. If she's in the woods, then maybe I can shoo her out."

Giving her a piercing look from under his white eyebrows, Grandpa said, "There's some mystery here, Maddy, you don't fool me. But I can tell you want to be on your own, so I'll just wait here. Just don't go too far and get lost."

"Thanks," she whispered. She wanted him to be quiet,

wanted everything to hush. The back of her neck prickled, and the tips of her fingers tingled. Something, something . . . Like a trace of red swirling in water, something was in the woods; she could feel it.

"OK, OK," Grandpa whispered, as if he knew their voices were too loud. "But don't be too long, or I will worry and come after you."

Maddy plunged into the knee-high wet grass and looked back. Standing tall and calm in his blue work shirt, Grandpa seemed like a lighthouse she could always see in the deepest darkness. He waved at her, grinning, as she went through the field, grass slapping her jeans. When she came to an aspen grove, Maddy darted under the branches and walked softly over the moss. Moisture soaked into her shoes. Mist dripped on her bare neck, down her back. She hardly noticed.

Going deeper into the woods, Maddy began to run. Branches slapped her face, but she had to get away from the road and its sounds. The last car horn faded into the distance, and all Maddy heard was the tocking of a chipmunk and the trees dripping. She ran on, only stopping when a sudden, sweet, wild cry curled through the woods, calling to her, the sound so sweet she thought her heart might shrivel and whirl to dust if she did not hear it again. Through a stand of birches, under a great oak, on to a dark pine she ran.

Again the cry fluted through the woods. This time it

coiled into her ears and rested on top of her heart. Maddy felt as if silver flowed through her veins, and she stopped to listen for the call again. Nothing. She ran to another stand of birch and pine, feeling the moss move under her feet. Pressing a hand to her chest, Maddy halted and heard the echo of many songs, as if someone had struck each tree to give off a ringing note. The forest began to move. Trees shook their leaves and bowed. The birch tree on her left danced and swayed.

Maddy sucked in a breath and tried to move, but her feet seemed plunged too deep in the moss. Her heart beat so hard it thundered in her ears. Looking down, she saw something gray and small and fierce, some sort of animal standing on its hind legs, peering up at her with a narrow face and bright eyes. Was it a weasel?

But then the creature stepped forward, and Maddy saw it had two legs, two arms, and a smooth face under a skin cap. And out of its mouth came these clear words: "I expected a cat, not a human being!"

CHAPTER ELEVEN

"You." The small voice wafted up to Maddy. "You are the one who lived with my cat."

Maddy did not speak, so excited that her mouth dropped open and tears came to her eyes. *What did the creature mean about a cat?*

It began to walk around her, tugging at its hat. "Two legs, two arms, a giant face—mouth like a cavern—words spill out of it—oof, that smell." It coughed and strode away from her, turning and holding its arms tightly across its chest.

"What smell?" burst out of her before she could think.

It fled for the nearest birch. The only way Maddy knew the creature was there was by the trembling of the green leaves. The trees around the glade shimmered and moved, vibrating with light and a strange wind.

Maddy clapped her arms to her chest. *Who is this? What is this?* She crouched down, peering through the leaves.

"Hush, I won't hurt you," she whispered. She knew now that sudden or loud noises frightened it. How could she get this creature to come out again? She sat on the grass and pulled her knees up. To calm both of them, she began to sing a tune Daddy played on his piano. It was one of Bach's pieces, and she formed the notes, remembering the way Daddy's hands flew over the keys, making music like rain.

The leaves parted. A frightened face poked through. Its eyes gleamed like thistle seeds, and Maddy could see a small, open mouth. Creeping out through the leaves, it stood before her. As Maddy sang, it began to turn and wave its arms under the music, as if bathing in a waterfall. For a moment, she thought the creature glowed silver. She stopped singing, and it stopped moving. Not *it,* she thought suddenly. *He.* With his pants and tunic, bow strapped to his back, and sharp-angled face.

"Oh, don't stop, don't stop!" He held out his arms. "I

did not know humans could make music like that, like rain, like birdsong."

So Maddy sang some more, dredging out of her memory the notes that seemed to calm this small being and make him happy.

"Sala lied to us," he said finally, when she ran out of music. "He said humans don't know about beauty or the songs of the world. But this is like the song of the snow geese returning." He opened his mouth:

> Onward, onward,
> home to nest,
> north to the circled lake.
> Watch how my wings curve,
> watch how my feathers swim
> in the wild winds of home.

"And you"—he waved at her—"you heard my call. Humans are not supposed to hear that."

Maddy nodded. "I had to come, it was so beautiful. It touched my heart."

"Heart." The creature nodded. He placed his hand over his chest, over the middle. "Elves have hearts, too."

"Elves!" she whispered. "I should have known. But they tell us there are no such things!"

"Ha!" The elf took off his hat and pulled at his hair.

Silver sparks jumped into the air, and a birch tree to their left began to jiggle and dance.

"Shhh," Maddy whispered, "something is happening."

"It is my anger." The elf pulled on his hat again. "My one great failing, along with my curiosity." He swung his arms rapidly. "Who *dares* to say there are no elves? Who dares to say that?" He strode about the clearing, muttering and popping his fingers. Each time, a silver spark jumped out and rose into the sky. Birds gathered above, swooping and diving, gobbling up the lights as they soared upward.

Maddy began to cry. She could not help it. Birds diving after elf sounds. An elf in front of her, talking! He stopped pacing and looked at her, wonderingly. He came and stood near, holding out his hands. One of her tears splashed onto his hand, and he cupped it to his face, sniffing.

"I can smell"—he paused—"I can smell your sadness. You think you are alone, that there is no one like you in the world. I think that sometimes." He let the tear fall onto the moss.

Suddenly, he tore his hat off and frowned. "What am I doing? I wanted to speak with a human, but now what will happen to me?" He opened his mouth and sent out a note of blue so deep it was almost black. It did not soar into the air but lifted above his head and stayed for a while, vibrating softly.

Maddy felt even sadder when she heard that sound. It made her think of a lone wolf howling on a ridge, of one swan riding off on a great wave into fearsome seas, of an eagle soaring so high it could never get down again.

She stretched out her arms. "What do you mean—what will happen to you? What is wrong?"

All life seemed to have gone out of the elf. He slumped to the ground, and his skin was pale as snow. "We are not allowed to be seen by humans. It would be bad enough for me to *see* a human; Sala could forgive that. He would just scold me and give me hard tasks to do. But to let myself be seen. And to talk to a human!"

"What will happen?" Maddy repeated again, wiping her nose on her sleeve.

"I will be cast out. I will have to live on my own in the forest. I will have to say good-bye to my love, Hele. And now that The Horned One is about? I will be eaten alive, *hislin* in my veins or no!"

"What is *hislin*, and who is The Horned One?" Maddy asked softly.

"What does it matter?" The elf sat on the moss and moaned, rocking his body back and forth. "I have lost everything! And all because of my curiosity!"

Maddy remembered a picture on Grandpa's bedroom wall, of Adam and Eve being cast out of paradise. Mourning, they fled the gates; mouths open in howls, they left love and light and deathless life.

"Couldn't you just not tell the other elves about seeing me?"

He spat, and a red larkspur sprang up through the moss. "Elves cannot lie. A lie stinks on our skin, like rotten meat. Anyone could smell it."

"Then let me come with you." Maddy rose suddenly, forgetting that Grandpa waited for her on the road. "If everyone sees me, then no one can be banished."

He stepped back, clutching his chest again. "You could not get past the watchers in the woods. They would alert the camp, and everyone would be gone by the time we arrived."

She chewed on her lower lip. She *had* to help him. "Come home with me, then. Grandpa is a wise man. He will know what to do."

"No, human child, even though you heard me singing—and that is a wonder, indeed—I cannot live with humans. I must go home and see what will happen." He disappeared into the shadows, and the trees quieted. The forest seemed darker now.

"Oh." Maddy sat down on the moss again, shaken and exhausted. Everything she knew about life was suddenly broken into pieces, like the bright shards in a kaleidoscope. Telephones, computers, homework, buses, everything was utterly changed now that the world had elves in it. And how could she hear his song and see the deep blue note of his sadness? What did that mean about *her*?

Far away, as if from another country, she heard her name. "Ma-dee! Maddy! Where are you? It's getting late."

She stood quickly, remembering Grandpa. She tried to run through the trees to him, but her knees would not work, and her feet slipped on the moss. Holding on to the trunks for balance, she dragged herself toward the sound of his voice. When she saw his blue shirt through the mist and the trees, she stumbled forward, almost falling.

He grasped her in his arms and smoothed her hair. "Hush, it's all right, hush, pumpkin, everything's all right. The woods are a little scary in the fog, aren't they? And no Sabrina, hmmmm? Hush, everything's all right now."

But it was not all right, for now there was another secret between them. How could she tell Grandpa what had happened? She opened her mouth, but no words came. Had the elf put a spell on her so she could not talk about him? Maddy rubbed her nose in Grandpa's shirt. He took her hand, and they set off through the woods for home.

CHAPTER TWELVE

As they walked slowly through the woods, Maddy
held Grandpa's hand. He hummed, as if the comforting
sound might lessen the strangeness of the mist and the
silence. She shook her head at him, and he stopped humming. Any sound, any *human* sound, startled her, prickling
along her arms and up her back.

They went through the aspen grove, the silver birches,
past the pine, and the woods began to thin out. Maddy
had no idea how long she'd been gone; a minute, an hour,
a whole day? And *where* had she been? It had seemed out

of time and place. Stumbling on some moss, Maddy caught a fragment of song. She stopped, and Grandpa stopped with her.

"What is it, pumpkin?"

She shook her head again, unable to speak. But she'd heard it, she had! Within the song were soft words about "roots" and "green heads." Then a bird called nearby, its voice suddenly rich and full of meaning. There was an echo in it, something new and strange. "Summers come and go," the bird sang, "warmth and clouds and"—here the call became incomprehensible. Maddy listened as hard as she could, standing absolutely still. Were there other words? "New life . . . soft nests," and then the call changed into notes that fell and swooped about her. She hugged Grandpa's arm tightly, and he stroked her head.

"What is it? What happened, Maddy? You're like someone who's seen the Pied Piper." He shook her shoulder gently. "Is it Sabrina? Did you see something, or did something frighten you?"

Maddy tried to push the words out through her lips, which felt stiff and unwieldy as wood. "No . . . no, Grandpa." He hugged her again, and the only words she could manage were "all right . . . I'm all right."

But she wasn't. She felt as if someone had peeled off the top of her head, stuck a spoon in, and stirred it, hard. Everything was mixed up inside, nothing was settled. Fragments of song spun around in her mind. She saw the face of the elf: small, fierce, and wary. He did not trust her. And why should he? Maddy thought. If other people saw an elf they would call the local television station, or write a book about it. Maybe they would even try to capture one and make money from him somehow.

Grandpa led her forward through the tall, wet grass. He joked, "Won't need to take a bath tonight, Maddy. Too bad I didn't bring some soap. Now, you mustn't worry. I'm sure Sabrina will turn up soon, howling for food and ready to sleep next to you."

Maddy hardly heard him. The words floated off over her head like milkweed silk on the wind. The only word she really heard was "Sabrina," though she had almost forgotten the cat was lost. But what had the elf meant by, "You lived with my cat"? *My cat?*

She'd have to go back tomorrow to see if he was still there. The elf said he couldn't go home again, whatever home was. Maybe he would be lonely and need a friend. Suddenly, she wondered about the saddle she'd found yesterday and tucked under her bed. What if the saddle belonged to *him?* It might be something she could bring back, and he would see how she could help him. Now that she knew elves existed, she could not let him go. She would search and search until she found him again.

As they stepped out onto the road, the setting sun burst through the mist. A yellow beam caught on oak leaves, fragmenting into silver, red, blue, and a deep, glowing green. She stopped, sucking in a breath. Grandpa halted beside her, still holding her hand.

"What is it, Maddy?"

She shivered and pulled her hand to her side.

"What do you see?" He turned to her and suddenly exclaimed, "Maddy, there must be a trick of light in this forest. It looks like moonlight shining on your face!" Shaking his head, he took up her hand again, and led her down the road.

CHAPTER THIRTEEN

Nata listened to the girl crashing away through the
underbrush. Had the scrolls talked about how *noisy* humans
were? And that smell! Nata sniffed his hands and coughed
violently. Her odor was on his skin. Even if he *could* lie,
that smell would give him away. Everyone would know
he had been among humans.

Nata clutched his arms around his chest. What would
he do? Sala would never let him return; he was strict about
the old rules. Nata moaned, and a purple note rose into

the air, following him. *I am walking like an ancient one,* Nata thought as he dragged his feet over the moss.

There, hidden in the pine thicket, was the cat he'd called only a sunrise ago, the same cat that had belonged to the human child. He'd almost forgotten that he'd come to the glade again to call another mount. Then he would have a backup cat if this one did not train easily. Sighing, he slipped a bridle over her head, soothing her as she jumped sideways.

"Hush, hush, my one, you will be my fine mount." Reaching into his bag, he took out some *tileen* and slipped the berries into her mouth. When she was done chewing, he mounted, pressed his knees into her sides, and gripped the reins. Would she break easily to the tack? He had only ridden her once before, and he still had not put on a saddle; she sidled as he chirruped to her.

A low branch slapped his cheek. "Mother of the forest! Watch where you're going!" he scolded himself. He rubbed his cheek and let blackness roll over him. Home. Gone forever. Now he could never join with Hele and have elf children light as thistledown. And all because of that human with her huge hands and sad face. Why hadn't he fled when he'd first heard her crashing through the forest?

He shook his head and pulled in on the reins. The cat slowed her pace and carefully picked her way around a large rock. It was *his* fault he would be banished, *his* fault that he would have to live on his own in the forest, and all because of his curiosity about humans. And what of The Horned One? How could he survive alone against Him?

Nata pulled his hat lower over his eyes, as if to cut out all sight of the future. Maybe he could travel to another elfin camp and join it. Hadn't Ela talked of the Shining River Clan and the Clan of the Cold Country? Good hunters were always needed, and Sala had just begun to teach him Far Seeing. Not many had the skill for that, Sala had said.

Nata sighed, and another deep purple note floated over his head, vibrating gently. His heart felt raw and sore as he imagined his friends in camp. As the day was ending, they would be sitting to share newly baked bread. Lele might strike up a song on her ashwood harp. Would Hele look for him, wondering where he was? They would not miss him yet; sometimes it took all day to find a new cat.

His mount jumped sideways as a pine branch slapped her ears. Nata pulled lightly on the reins and directed her around the tree. "Hush, hush," he soothed, "you are a fine cat, a brave one."

Brave. He would need more than bravery to survive on his own. Should he go back to camp and see if Sala would let him stay? Tell him all and then wait for his judgment? For Sala was a wise leader, a gentle leader.

Suddenly, he was seized by a longing so fierce and

sharp that he called out. A black note spun up into the darkening sky. He felt as if a knife had ripped through his flesh, dividing him in half, and that part of him lay on the forest floor. He'd heard stories of elves who had disobeyed the laws and had to live on their own in the forest. Without the special birch brew, without the songs and stories, those elves had withered to gray wraiths, wandering the forest, their wits askew.

Hele. He saw her with her hair shaken out in the wind like a silver cloud foretelling rain. He missed her so much that another cry rose from him, and his mount sprang forward. As Nata keened again, his sorrow lifted into the sky like a fierce, black bird.

Somewhere, not too far away, Hele heard and, for a second, stopped breathing. She knew Nata was in trouble and summoned the others. "I just heard Nata! Something terrible has happened to him!"

Nata's cries sliced through the air and went deep into the ears of the great horned owl. He shook His feathers into a great ruff and pulled them tight again. Opening His beak, He cried out for the hunt. The elves heard and raced for their bows and arrows. The call shivered down Nata's back. Chirruping to his mount, he raced through the woods.

Chapter Fourteen

Where could he hide? He was only one elf against The Horned One, and Nata knew he could not win that kind of battle. It would take many warrior elves to vanquish this one! Setting the cat at a fast pace through the forest, Nata worried that his new mount might be prey for the owl as well. For a moment he thought of heading toward camp, but he did not want to lead The Horned One to the other elves. He'd need to find a hollow tree, a place where he and the cat could hide from those deadly talons.

His mount slipped on some wet leaves, and Nata steadied her with pressure from his knees.

The cry came again, nearer this time. Nata could hear blood in it, could hear the fierce hunger of it.

> *Talons grip tight,*
> *beak tear through,*
> *elf, elf, I come for you!*

screamed The Horned One.

Nata's hair stood on end. He charged through the forest, the owl's cry winging at his back. Needles whipped his face as that cry sang in his veins: "I come for you!" With horror, he saw again his mother disappearing into the sky and, later, his father seized by the same great talons.

Through the dark mist he spurred the cat, her feet slipping on wet moss. Fog blew through his hair, and in his fear, his hair glowed silver, trailing sparks of light like an exploding firecracker. Birds woke and cried out. Squirrels in the high branches screamed to one another.

Nata urged the cat forward, but he could feel her weariness. In spite of her fear, she didn't have the stamina for this kind of race. She began to slow, and at that moment, the owl swept nearer. Though Nata could not see Him, he sensed the shadow hurtling across the forest floor.

Sides heaving, mouth open, the cat stopped under a

pine. Nata jumped off and tugged on her reins. "Quickly, quickly!" He pushed through the underbrush, scanning the tree trunks for a hiding hole. But there was none.

The owl pierced the air with His hateful cry, beating through the branches. Nata felt warmth streaming out of His open mouth, smelled the rank odor of carrion.

"Aiee!" Suddenly, Nata was so angry he lifted slightly above the moss. He heard his mother's cries again; he heard the fat voice of the owl after He had fed to the full. Coming to ground again, Nata pulled out his silver knife and braced his back against a stiff branch.

Then the wings were overhead, beating against the foggy air. The Horned One dove toward him, wings enfolding. Nata slashed upward, but missed. As one hooked talon sliced Nata's shoulder, he felt *hislin* rushing out of his veins. Rising, the owl cried out again, then swept downward. Gusts of hot, stinking air flowed over Nata, and he screamed as the owl landed on him, pinning him to the ground. Looking up into one golden eye, Nata saw a fierce hunger. The owl's beak snapped closer. Nata tried to stab the owl's belly, but his arm was trapped.

Then something wild and fearsome yowled in front of him. A black shape hurtled at the owl, slashing with her claws. The owl jumped back, releasing Nata, and snapped at the cat's nose. Spinning away, the cat jumped on the owl's back, away from taloned feet and ripping beak. At the same time, Nata stabbed deep into the owl's soft underbelly. The great bird screamed and rose heavily into the air, disappearing through the trees. Nata gripped his wounded shoulder, then looked at his cat. She was hurt, too, with blood flowing down her face.

"Come, quickly, He might return. Come." He knew the wound he'd given the owl was not severe, for no blood had spurted out. Holding the reins, he ran with the cat through the underbrush to a fallen log. He pushed aside the leaves and ferns and crawled into the middle of the large log, pulling the cat after.

"Good girl, brave girl," he sang to her, "you saved my life."

Once they were safely hidden, he turned and touched her face, crying out as her blood burned him. Shivering, he felt his shoulder, the hole made by the owl's talon. Cupping his hand, he collected *hislin* as it flowed and rubbed it into the cat's face. The sliced skin above her nose seamed together, and fur grew quickly over it.

Then Nata held the edges of his own wound closed. As the *hislin* pooled behind his skin, it knitted the hole and the flow stopped. But though the hole was closed, Nata still felt an ache inside where the tip of the talon had dug, as if a piece of blood from another animal were lodged there.

"Hush, brave one, you will be well." He smoothed the cat with his hand, singing a song into her ear about living long, with the joy of the hunt forever before her.

She slept, purring, while he kept awake for a time yet, seeing those deadly talons and feeling once again the owl's warm, bloody breath. What if the owl attacked the camp? What if He went for Hele? Nata ground his teeth. How could he get back to warn them?

A loneliness so deep took him that he cried, silver tears sliding down the black fur of the cat. When they fell to the ground, small silver mushrooms grew. Finally, Nata slept, head pillowed in the cat's side.

CHAPTER FIFTEEN

Maddy lay in bed looking up at the ceiling, how the morning light shone on the plastered surface. There was a hump just like a rhinoceros about to charge, and one patch of shadow looked like a racing cat.

Cat. Elf. Maddy hugged her arms close, and a thread of song began in her head. It came unbidden, from some unknown place. She could not tell the words—they were in a silvery tongue she did not understand. But sounds fluted up and down, sending shivers along her backbone. *Such beauty in the world,* she thought, *such wonder.* The song seemed to promise things she could almost name. If she forgot about words and just let pictures come to mind, there were images and colors: green leaves shifting against the sun, silver clouds sailing across the moon, a stream running through a clearing with small figures sitting near a fire. They were singing, and the notes that rose from their mouths were golden, like small suns over their heads.

Maddy hugged her arms to her chest, a little afraid. It was wonderful, this magic, but a little frightening, too. These pictures and sounds floating up out of—where? And what was she to *do* with them? Maddy sighed, swung her feet out of bed, and dressed. Daddy always said that music made him see pictures in his mind; maybe this was a little like what he saw, except—magic. Today, she vowed, she would find her elf, if she had to hike through the whole of the woods behind that ice-cream stand. But would Grandpa let her go on her own? This was *her* elf, *her* secret, just as her parents had silver picture frames around their special moments.

When Maddy went downstairs, Grandpa was sitting at the table sipping coffee from his blue mug.

"Well, now I *am* worried," he said, looking up. "Sabrina's been away a whole day, and that isn't like her. I wonder if she did go off with that tom."

With a jolt, Maddy remembered. Sabrina. Was she in the forest? Had she somehow been found by the elf? He *had* mentioned a cat. Maddy would search for her magic creature, and maybe he would know where Sabrina was.

"Let's see if we can find her this morning, Grandpa," Maddy said, pouring granola into a bowl.

"Where? Any ideas?" He fiddled with the handle of his cup.

"Down near the ice-cream stand. But I want to go by myself, Grandpa," she added quickly.

He peered at her and rubbed his mustache. "Secrets, Maddy? Yesterday when I came to get you you looked as if you'd seen a ghost!"

"I wasn't afraid, Grandpa, just . . ." Maddy couldn't finish, couldn't even find the right words.

"Just what?" He thought for a moment and then said, "All right, have your secrets. Everyone needs a secret now and then. But I want to find our cat." He stood and got out their backpacks. Into them he put snacks, a roll of tape each, a flashlight, bandages, and a small towel.

"Why the towel, Grandpa?"

"In case she's hurt and we have to carry her back in a sling."

"She's not hurt—I know she's not hurt. Maybe lost. Maybe something. But not hurt."

"How do you know?"

"I just do. Where will you look?"

Grandpa shrugged the pack onto his back. "I'm going to hunt through our woods. Once before she went off with some tom, and maybe that happened this time. Are you riding down to the ice-cream stand on your bike, Maddy?"

She grinned, happy that Grandpa was letting her go off on her own. "Yes, thank you, Grandpa!" Rising, she shrugged into the backpack he held out for her.

"Come home by noon, pumpkin. That's enough time by yourself. Your parents . . ." He left the words unsaid.

"They wouldn't mind, Grandpa, honest! I often go places on my own in the city, and it's lots more dangerous than the country." She opened the door and stood on the top step.

"Maybe," said Grandpa, "maybe. Just be careful. If anything happens to you, my daughter'll have my hide!"

Maddy paused for a moment; her parents seemed faint and far away. What would they think if she told them she'd seen an elf? Would they believe her? Would Grandpa?

He bounded down the steps and pointed at his watch. "Remember, Maddy, keep track of the time. I want you back here by twelve o'clock."

"Right. See you later." Maddy pulled her bike away from the side of the house, mounted, and sped down the driveway to the road.

Maddy parked her bike by the ice-cream stand and ran up the lane, over the bridge. She did not call for Sabrina, afraid the noise might frighten the elf. Coming to the field she'd gone through yesterday, she paused at the edge.

What were her chances, really, of finding the elf in these woods? But she had to start someplace, so she pushed through the drying grass toward the pine and birches. In a while, she found the spot where she had crouched yesterday. Kneeling, she touched the moss with her fingertips. A thin, small note rose, then stopped.

She sucked in a breath. Was the whole world full of song? Did everything have a song: birds, leaves, moss, and sky? What would happen to *her* if every time she touched something music rose up? Carefully, Maddy stepped toward a silver birch and stroked the bark. A faint tinkling sound came out. She backed away, flinging her arms across her chest. Overhead, a robin flew, carrying something home to its nest. She heard the raucous peeps of the baby birds. But when she listened, eyes closed, the peeping changed into something else:

> *Mine—this time!*
> *My worm!*
> *Shove over!*

Then the words disappeared, and the sounds became hungry birds chirping. Shaking her head, Maddy strode forward. She knew how to get out of the woods, had all the landmarks set in her mind—the big pine, the aspen grove, the birches, the clearing. As she went deeper through the trees, the air hushed and became still. There were no sounds from the road.

She lifted her head and sniffed. There was something in the wind, a hot, red scent, a danger smell. Hairs prickled along her arms and legs. Blindly, trusting to this strange new instinct, Maddy pushed through the woods. As she went along, there was a faint new smell, metallic and sharp. She thought it was like fear, and hurried faster. On through a grove of birches where bark hung in tight rolls. On across a bed of moss so thick her feet sank out of sight. On through a clearing where the ferns rose and stretched toward the sun. A small twittering came from the ferns.

Then the odor grew sharper. Maddy coughed and stopped. In the distance a stream rustled; a crow called from a near pine. She thought she heard the word "death." Covering her face for a moment, Maddy breathed in the warmed air of her cupped hands. But only for a moment. If she wanted to see her elf again, she *had* to keep going.

She came to a place where the woods felt broken and torn. The air had a red tinge to it, like red dye trailed through clear water. The leaves were scumbled and messed, and above hung the smell of blood. She tried to breathe shallowly, in small bursts. She coughed and shivered, goose bumps pimpling her skin. Then a cat meowed.

Looking down, Maddy saw a fallen log with an open end. She knelt and peered inside. There were four eyes shining in the darkness, staring back at her.

"You!" came a soft voice. "Human child, you found us!" The elf stumbled out into the clearing to stand before her.

"How did you make your way through the wood? You humans have more secrets than I ever knew," he chattered, "singing, rescuing, wait until Sala hears of this." He paused and rubbed his face. "But Sala will not hear of it because I cannot go back and tell him."

"What happened to you?" Maddy asked. Her skin was still covered with goose bumps, and the odor of blood clouded her nose.

"Attack," he said briefly. "The Horned One came after me yesterday. And He would have eaten me, too, except my cat saved me!" He pulled on a leather strap, drawing out a black cat with a matted coat.

"Sabrina!" Maddy exclaimed. "She looks terrible! How did you find her? And why is she with you?"

"She is mine now. I caught her. I am training her." The elf moved closer to the cat and stroked her ears.

"She *was* mine," Maddy said softly, "my special cat at Grandpa's house."

The elf bowed and said politely but firmly, "That may be so, but now she belongs to me. I have healed her wound with *hislin,* and we are bound together until she dies."

It was all too sudden; she could not take in losing her cat and finding the elf at the same time. So she asked a question instead. "You said *hislin.* What is that?"

"It is elf blood," he answered.

Maddy knelt by Sabrina. "Oh, Sabrina, are you all right?" She held out a hand and gently stroked the cat, who butted against Maddy's hand and began to purr. Tears came to Maddy's eyes.

"You can't," she choked, "you can't just *take* her. She belongs with me." She tried to hug Sabrina close, but the cat pulled away.

"Already?" Maddy exclaimed. "Already she will go to you?" Sitting down, Maddy put her hands to her face and cried. "All year I look . . . forward to Sabrina . . . She always waits for me . . . on the top step," she said between sobs.

The elf just stood there, watching. Maddy did not see the deep blue note vibrating above his head. But she felt, obscurely, that he sympathized with her; something in the air seemed to ring with her loss.

"She was," Maddy faltered, "she was . . ."

"Your friend?" offered the elf. "We call a friend *aleeno*."

"Yes," said Maddy, sniffing and wiping her nose.

"A friend is like a partner," mused the elf. "Once humans and elves were partners—so the ancient scrolls say."

"We were?" Maddy lifted her head from her knees. "When? And what did we do?"

"Oh, a long time ago." The elf waved his hand airily. He took his cap off, smoothed his hair back, and looked up at the sky. "We cannot stay here. Another night alone in the forest might kill me, *hislin* in my veins or no. Do you think . . ." His voice trailed off and disappeared into the moss, which chirped faintly and moved beneath Maddy's feet.

"Do I think *we* could be partners?" Maddy's thoughts leapt ahead. As the elf ducked his head and winced, Maddy tried to speak more softly. "Partners help each other when they are in trouble. I can help you. I have your saddle at home, at least I think it is your saddle."

"Is it green?" he asked eagerly. "With red designs of the forest around its edge?"

Maddy nodded, and the elf came up and put his hand on her knee. To Maddy, it felt like a shaft of sunlight. "I was in trouble for letting my other cat run away with its bridle and saddle on. Sala will be so happy to hear . . ." He stopped.

Maddy rose carefully. She knew sudden movements startled the elf; she also thought her smell offended him, for he kept wrinkling his nose.

"Come home with me. I know," she said, putting out a hand. "I know it is not your *real* home. But just until you know what you're going to do; just to be safe from the owl."

The elf looked at her, then at the cat. Pulling off his cap again, he stretched his hair out until silver sparks jumped into the air. Two birds swooped down and gobbled them up. Maddy couldn't help gasping, and the elf stepped back. Then he rubbed his whole face thoroughly, looking up at her as if he hoped she had disappeared.

"I'm still here," she said calmly.

He surveyed her from her feet to her head, shivered, gave a quiet nod, and said, "All right, human child, I will come with you just for a while, until I go back to camp and see if Sala will let me stay. I do not know about being partners, but we are *aleeno,* friends."

Mounting Sabrina, he took up the reins, and Maddy recognized with a shock that her cat was bridled the same as the tomcat who had run away.

CHAPTER SIXTEEN

Maddy walked beside the elf through the woods. For a long time they did not say anything. Once Sabrina chirruped and sidled against Maddy's leg. The elf pulled gently on the rein. Smiling, Maddy noted that Sabrina would still come to her.

"We must be careful, human child," the elf said softly. "I must not be seen, even though most humans cannot *see* elves. They think we are a shred of mist, a falling leaf, a patch of sunlight."

His voice felt like silver in her ears; it ran down inside

her body, soothing her, quieting her heart. She walked even more slowly.

"We'll be careful," she answered.

After a while, they came through the grove of trees where the road snaked in and out of shadow. The elf pulled Sabrina to a halt. "That—is a human road. I have never been on one before." He sucked in a breath and pulled his cap low over his eyes.

"It's all right, really it is. If we keep to the side of the road, you can always just disappear if anyone comes. But no one walks here because no one walks, that's what Grandpa says!" Maddy realized she was babbling and stopped. *I mustn't get too excited,* she thought. *I must not frighten him by moving too fast or talking too loud.*

The elf took in another breath, urging Sabrina forward. They stepped out onto the road, with the elf crouching low over the cat's neck. Silently, they went down the dusty way; only wind and the faraway water disturbed the quiet. Finally, the elf rose from his crouching position and looked up at Maddy.

"What is your name, child? Humans *do* have names, don't they? I think Sala told us that."

"Of course I have a name," she answered. "It's Maddy. Short for Madeline."

"That is a pretty name," he said. "Madd-ee is like the mud we dig up from the summer ponds to put on our gardens. It means something rich and fruitful."

Maddy asked, "Are you allowed to tell me your name?"

He rubbed the cat's shoulder and coughed. "Elfin names are special. They are part of us. I cannot give it to you lightly, human child. Every elf has an outer name and an inner one, although I have not earned my inner one yet. My outside name is Nata."

"Nata," she repeated softly.

He shivered slightly when she said his name, then went back to something they had talked about earlier in the woods. "Maybe that is how a partnership began—with elves and humans. Maybe it began with names, giving them to each other." He paused.

"Like presents," Maddy put in. "A name is like a gift."

He looked up at her and smiled. Suddenly, the sky seemed bluer, and out of the corner of one eye, Maddy saw a bird so golden it looked like a falling sun.

"I think," Nata said, "I think that if you can help me, I will help you—as we used to in the faraway green land where we once lived. If we are partners, like that"—he held up two twined fingers—"then I shall give you your true name, your inner name."

"And then?" she asked quietly.

"Then you will be able to hear all the songs of the world, Madd-ee."

"I already can, at least some of them, Nata. This morning I heard some baby birds arguing about who should get the next worm, and I heard a faint song from some tree bark and moss." She looked sideways at him.

He pushed his hat back in surprise. "So *soon* you hear that? I wonder if you can hear songs because you have talked with me. Although"—he tugged on one earlobe and frowned—"I think there is more to it than that. Maybe, Madd-ee, a long time ago our families were joined, or you were linked with an elfin family. And that is why the songs are in your ears."

Maddy nodded. She didn't know what Nata was saying when he talked of the long-ago green land. All she knew was it sounded like paradise, and he was offering her something so special, so unique that there was no other person on earth who had it.

"I am honored." She stopped and bowed slightly to Nata. She thought that being with him was a little like walking with the queen of England, and she should observe the same courtesies. Then they came to the spot before the bridge where Maddy had left her bike.

"Nata?" She pointed to the ditch. "There is my bike for riding on, just as you have Sabrina to ride." She picked up her bike and began to push it over the packed dirt. She would go too fast if she mounted, and Maddy wasn't sure how Nata would react to this great, lumbering machine right beside him.

He nudged Sabrina forward with his knees and began

to mutter, his mood shifting to something darker, bleaker. "I am a fool, going with a human child, near people this way. Sometimes tales tell of elves who lose their minds, wandering unseeing through the forest." He turned toward her.

"Oh, no, no, you are not losing your mind. It's just that you've never talked with a person before, and I imagine it is"—she paused—"a little scary."

"Scary," he muttered as Sabrina paced forward. "Scary is The Horned One, not a human girl. If I can fight an owl, surely I can talk with a human!" He squared his shoulders and sat higher in the saddle.

"You are very brave, indeed, to fight a great horned owl, Nata. Grandpa says they can rip cats apart. Even skunks!"

Luckily, there were thick stands of trees bordering the road all the way to Grandpa's house, so Nata could stay in the shadows while Maddy walked her bike beside him. Only two cars passed them, and Nata had hidden himself long before the cars approached. When they got to the field below Grandpa's house, Maddy left her bike at the grass's edge and led Nata across the meadow.

"That's where I live—in the summer." She pointed to the white building ahead of them. Suddenly, she wanted to leap and laugh and run. Here she was, Maddy Trevor, ten years old, of New York City, talking with an elf!

"You live inside a box?" Nata slowed the cat so they were barely moving through the tall grasses of the field. "With no air or sun or birdsong?"

"A house." She nodded. "You can stay with us—I suppose you'll have to be inside for safety."

Suddenly, Nata spat into the grass, and a red flower sprang up. Maddy jumped back. "I cannot live inside that box!" He pointed a shaking finger. "There must be another place I can be—safe from The Horned One."

Maddy ached for him, to protect and keep him from danger. Maybe this was part of being partners, keeping each other from harm.

"I know!" she said suddenly and loudly. Nata disappeared. She could not see him, though she searched and searched as Sabrina crouched in the grass.

"Oh, Nata, come back, I didn't mean to be so loud. I'm sorry."

Slowly a brown face poked through the grass. She felt something soft but strong circling inside her head. It said:

Quiet, calm,
no anger, no sudden
leaps, no sudden
questions, quiet,
calm, rest.

It was like a river flowing through her veins, light and gleaming. She began to hum to herself, the faint notes from

Daddy's playing, from a Bach prelude. The music seemed to call Nata out of his hiding place. For he rose up out of the grass and listened, smiling.

"Oh, I would give much to hear the whole of that song. How beautiful it is!" he exclaimed.

And quietly, restfully, Maddy remembered how lovely her parents' music was. It was something that flowed and ran like a shining river, just as her thoughts now seemed to move like water. Maybe the magic that was in her elf was somehow in music as well? Maddy wondered. Suddenly, she remembered something Grandpa had said when he told her about the woman and her lover fleeing down the dirt road. He'd said that anything was worth it to feel "this singing in her veins." Now she knew what he meant; there was singing in *her* veins, and she would do anything to keep it there.

Maddy held out her hands. "You did that. You made me calm, made my thoughts go like water."

"I think"—he paused—"I think I am beginning to get a name for you."

She leaned forward eagerly. "But not yet"—he waved a hand at her—"not quite yet, young one. Now, what are we to do?"

She felt honored to be asked her opinion. "I know," she said calmly. "The tree house. It has a roof—no owl could get at you there. There is a door you can close, but it has small windows to let in air, sunlight, and the songs of birds. That is what you want, isn't it?"

"Well, it is not what I *want,* but it is better than being in the forest waiting for The Horned One to devour me." He sighed. "Let us go then."

Maddy led the way forward through the meadow, over the cut grass to the butternut tree. Pointing to the ladder, she said, "You can go up there. I'll get you some moss for a bed, if you like, and something to drink. What do elves eat?"

"Berries, vegetables, and water will do."

"Do you want to meet my grandfather, Nata? He is a wise man and could help us." Maddy wasn't sure if she wanted to keep Nata to herself or share him with Grandpa. Was Grandpa even home yet? He had gone out to the woods to search for Sabrina. How long ago that all seemed!

"Not today." Nata sighed and began to climb the nailed wood up to the tree house. "One human a day is enough for me." He laughed slightly, to soften the words, and Maddy smiled up at him.

When she brought back a small basket of blueberries, raw beans, a cup of water, and some moss, Nata did not notice her. He was sitting at the door of the tree house, staring toward the woods, and he was calling out some-thing in a language she did not know. But she saw that the notes were a deep blue and that they lifted heavily into the air, blowing slowly in the wind past the tall pines.

CHAPTER SEVENTEEN

All through the night Nata lay on the soft moss in the tree house, with the door firmly closed. He turned and sighed as he slept, flinging out his arms and sweating. Dreams came: curved talons and the hot breath of an owl; Hele, holding out her arms to him; Sala, frowning. Then the wind turned, darkness shifted, and he woke suddenly to stare at the black ceiling. A bat twittered, homing in on a moth that fluttered outside the tree house door. It flew in the window and hid in a corner, where Nata shielded it with his breath.

Nata scowled. There was no one to shield him now. He was an outcast, gone. He could feel the *hislin* contract and falter in the inner chambers of his heart. His fingers grew cold, and his skin paled. *Outcast—gone.* But his people needed him! What if the great owl were attacking their camp at this very moment? They must have all warriors there to fend off The Horned One. What if the owl were to go after Hele?

He had a quick, frightening vision of Hele running with the owl after her. He clenched his hands and sucked in a breath. How could he stay here with Madd-ee? It was fine to talk about a partnership between an elf and a human family in the warm light of day. But *how* could they help?

His yearning for home was suddenly so great that he groaned. He wanted to breathe the air that came from other elves, soft, with a faint tinge of silver. He wanted to eat *risele* and the herbs that Hele brought home in a woven basket. He needed to sit in the circle of elves and pass the steaming cup, hearing Sala's stories of the past when the world was new and only elves walked over the green sward. If the food, the air, and the camp were all gone, Nata was sure he would turn into a wraith and disappear into the sky.

Shivering and clasping his hands to his chest, he watched dawn come. He was colder now that he had left the company of other elves. As the light glowed in the east, he whispered one word, *"condine,"* the name for the first light of dawn, when a red flush showed over the woods and the first bird woke and called. Nata stepped onto the platform outside the tree house and marked the last morning star in the east, a white point as chilled and lonely as he felt now.

When a robin sang above, Nata lifted his face.

Come, beaks,
open beaks,
eat sweet worms,
grow swift and sleek.

As the notes rained down, he turned slowly in the birdsong, rubbing his skin and face until he glowed silver. The birdsong stilled his loneliness for a moment, and he knew what he must do. Taking a deep breath, Nata jumped in one fluid motion from the tree to the ground, using his arms for balance. When his feet hit the ground, jolting his head, the thoughts were clear inside: *I will go home. I cannot live without other elves. I will take my chance with Sala. He must let me in, he must, for he needs every warrior he has!*

Sending out one clear, bell-like note, Nata watched and waited. Out of the shadows sprang a darker piece of shadow—his cat—moving easily. She showed no sign of her wounds from that terrible fight with the owl. Nata swung a leg over the cat and paused, scratching his hair until the sparks flew.

How could he leave just like that, after all Maddee's

kindness? He dismounted, ran to the ladder rungs nailed to the tree, and carved something quickly with his knife. The runes of his name sloped gracefully around the first rung; later they would catch the sunlight in their hollows and lines.

Mounting the cat again, Nata pressed in with his knees. He did not know if Sala would let him back in camp; he had no plan for what he would say. But he knew he must get home before The Horned One attacked again, and before he began to disintegrate.

CHAPTER EIGHTEEN

Low pine branches brushed Nata's face. As the sun edged over the hills, colors washed over him. Clouds flew through the sky, singing of cold Arctic floes and seas as still as glass. A goshawk perched in a high tree, snapping his beak and calling:

> *What will become of me?*
> *What, oh, what?*
> *My stomach is shrunken,*
> *my feet are clean of blood.*

Nata called out, "It is early still, beaked one. Two fields down, they will be haying. Listen for the harvester. Look for mice and voles and snakes."

The hawk ruffled his wings, shook his tail, and thanked him. With one swift motion, he lifted into the wind and flapped heavily off toward the fields.

When the sun was higher in the sky, Nata came to the bridge where the golden water rushed and rocks sang in the sun. Their song was a slow, ancient one. Nata could hear them calling with notes so low they barely vibrated.

We were here before you.
We were a river of fire,
then a river of stone.

As he passed over them, Nata bowed to the rocks. After all, compared to them he was a newcomer. He paused for a moment under a tall tree. No one would see the black cat in the darkness or the elf clothed in animal skins. Even a human who could *see* could not mark his utter stillness or smell him, but Nata knew that another elf could, now that he had been among humans. Something from the *laglan*'s breath and sweat clung to his skin, giving it a faint acrid tinge.

How will I get past the outposts? he wondered. Once, long ago, Sala had told about an elf child who clung to a weasel's belly when she ran away from her parents. The elf child had a wild adventure when the weasel raced between two sheets of ice. *If a weasel,* Nata thought, *why not a cat?* Her smell might cover his.

He jumped from the cat and crawled beneath her. Willing her quiet, he seized the fur, wishing she had a saddle strap to grip. Crying out, she jumped sideways, and he hushed her with a fragment of song. If he stayed just so, his feet were hidden. He could hold on to the head strap of the bridle from underneath. No one could see his hands or body. In his fierce longing to get back, Nata did not consider what the watchpost elves would make of a rider-less cat with a bridle on.

But after his mount had gone some distance, Nata realized the watchers in the forest would stop her. If he took off her tack, the elves would not bother her; they would just think her a cat wandering in the woods. Wrinkling his nose in disgust, Nata realized this was the closest he had ever come to lying.

Quickly, he took off the bridle, hiding it in a pine thicket and covering it with pine needles. Then he stroked the cat's head, crooning, "It is all right, lovely one. Only for a little time, I promise. Let me hold tight to your fur, and later I will give you a rubdown."

His cat nosed him and chirruped. He climbed under her again and clutched her neck fur. Bringing his knees up, he pressed a tuft of hair between them. He tucked his head under her throat, spoke to the cat, and she began to pace through the woods.

Through the beech trees they went, with the birches swaying and bending in greeting. He willed them away, telling them to hush their bright songs. He commanded the moss to lie still and the birds to say nothing. So the cat, with Nata under her, came to the first watchtower, high in an old pine.

Nata held his breath as his mount walked beneath the tree. She went through the shadows, and he heard the faint words, "A riderless cat. Let her pass."

He breathed out as the pine tree receded behind them. Clutching his mount tighter, he neared the oak tree of the second watch. His legs ached, but he kept them tightly gripped around the tuft of fur. The cat ambled slowly under the oak, nosing an acorn and sidling to the left after a dragonfly. Nata held on, his bottom almost hitting the moss, as he heard the whispered words, "Cat, no rider, let her by."

Hislin pumped faster through his veins. His stomach fluttered. Soon, soon, he would be home. The cat pushed through the forest, and Nata entered a half-dreaming state where the trees blurred green and all sounds were muted. What brought him out of that state was the sharp odor of smoke. He could smell elf brew and meat broth. There were children laughing and calling and Hele's clear voice in the background. Then he heard another voice, dark and sad.

"Keep looking," Sala said. "Keep asking the animals and

birds if they have seen Nata. He must be *somewhere,* unless that beast of the air has gotten him!"

He heard Hele cry out and the children stopped twittering. Nata pulled gently on the fur under his cat's throat, and Sabrina stopped.

"What is this?" Sala asked. "A riderless cat? Cala, is this one of the new mounts?"

For a moment, Nata stayed hidden, drinking in the words and smells. They soothed the awful loneliness that had threatened to devour him.

Nata let go of the cat, crawled out, and stood before the leader. "Sala." He held his hands up in supplication.

"Nata!" Hele hurried toward him. "We were so worried! We heard your call. What happened?"

Sala strode forward to give him a hug. He grasped Nata's hands and then dropped them suddenly. "What is this?" He shook his fingers vigorously. "The smell of *laglan* is on your skin. Oh, Nata, what have you done?"

"I let myself be seen by a human." He bowed to Sala. "She came upon me suddenly, and in truth, I wished to see her, though I know that is forbidden."

There were murmurs from the other elves as they gathered around. "Foolish, putting the whole camp in danger," someone rebuked him.

"I know I have done wrong, Sala," Nata went on. "But I have been punished. The Horned One came after me; I had to battle him on my own." He touched his shoulder where the claw had sunk in. "I almost lost, but my cat fought with the owl."

"That was brave," Hele said, reaching out to touch him. But Nata motioned her away. Not yet. Not until he knew what judgment Sala would give.

"And the human child, Madd-ee, helped me, gave me food. Sala, she *saw* me and *heard* my songs, as well as the songs of the forest. You said a human could not do that."

Sala came out of a deep reverie and shook his head. Rubbing his face wearily, he opened his mouth to let out one blue note of sorrow. "Oh, Nata, I wish it had been any other elf than you, whom I have loved, who has been learning Far Seeing."

Sala clasped his hands behind his back and walked in a tight circle. "Now the humans *know* that we are here in the woods. The entire camp will have to move, for you have put us all in danger." He flung up a hand and pointed. "I banish you from our camp and from elfin company. You must live on your own in the forest and never be with elves again."

The words punched him sideways, and Nata almost fell. The other elves gasped and rustled; small cries and groans floated up above the camp. "Banishment . . . forever . . . never before . . ."

Then Lele came and stood beside Sala. She whispered in his ear for a moment as Nata shivered and beads of dark sweat poured down his face.

Sala shook his head, then listened again as Lele said more words in his ear. Finally, he reached out and tapped Nata lightly on the shoulder. "My mate has convinced me that banishment is too harsh a punishment for one such as you. She has reminded me of a story in the scrolls; by performing a brave deed, an elf threatened with banishment was allowed back into camp. But you must leave us for a time, Nata. I have lost my trust in you, and it will take a while to get it back. You must show me in some way"—he waved his hand—"that you are worthy of my trust again." He touched Nata's cheek. "Do a great deed, and you can come back."

Where his finger had rested, there was a faint crescent moon. Nata bowed.

"I will perform such a deed, Sala, I promise, and I *will* come back." He nodded to the two leaders, mounted his cat, and disappeared into the shadows of the forest.

CHAPTER NINETEEN

When Maddy went down to breakfast the next morning, Grandpa was sipping coffee from his blue mug. He looked over its rim. " 'Lo, pumpkin."

Maddy beamed at him. "Sabrina's back." The rest of the words nudged to get out: "And there's an elf with her!" But she could not say them, not yet. For just a little while, she wanted to keep Nata all to herself.

"Well, *that's* good news. Where is she?" Grandpa took another sip and smiled.

"Outside." Again she was tempted to add, "with the elf who slept all night in the tree house, Grandpa!" But she did not. She felt him watching her, watching as she fidgeted in her seat. Suddenly, she bounced up and grabbed a basket, unable to wait any longer.

"I'm going to pick some berries for breakfast." Dancing on her toes, hardly able to wait, Maddy ran out to the drive to pick raspberries. After her basket was half full, she went to the butternut, grabbed the lower rung of the ladder, and climbed up the tree. Trying not to startle Nata, she slowed at the top rung and cautiously looked inside the tree house. Blinking her eyes after the sunlight, she saw nothing. She leaned forward, putting her head inside the tree house. Maybe he was in a corner, in the shadows.

Except for the moss, the room was empty. Where *was* Nata? Had he gone out to find food? Backing slowly down the ladder, Maddy wondered if he'd taken Sabrina on a ride somewhere. Maybe elves had rituals to start their day, and she would just have to learn them.

At the bottom of the tree, something glowed on the first rung of the ladder. Maddy saw beautiful letters curling around like a sweetbriar vine, holding pictures of nuts, berries, flowers. Light ran along the carvings like water over golden pebbles. She did not know what the letters said, but the air that rose from them was sad and final— like the last day of autumn. Maddy sat on the grass, clasping her knees to her chest and blinking her eyes. Nata had decided that she could not help and had gone back to camp, she knew. And when would she ever see him again?

The day seemed dimmed, as if the sunlight were filtered through a gray lens. Sounds were muted, and Maddy moved in a daze. Her elf was gone, before she'd even gotten a chance to know him, and he'd taken Sabrina with him. Hand resting on her knees, Maddy sat, unseeing, until sudden words startled her.

"Want to go for a bike ride, pumpkin?" Folding his long legs, Grandpa sat beside her on the grass. "You look sad. What's wrong?" He craned his neck and added, "Where's Sabrina?"

"That's it," she sniffed. "She's gone again." Maddy grabbed a hank of grass, twisting it through her fingers.

"But she just came back. I don't like this, Maddy, I don't like it at all. She's playing fast and loose with us," he joked.

Maddy could not answer; her lips felt stiff with loss, and only by a great effort could she keep from crying.

Grandpa put his arm around her, pulling her close until Maddy's head rested on his shoulder. "Don't you think she'll come back? She went off before and came home; why should this time be any different?"

Maddy shook her head and took in the pungent smell

of coffee from Grandpa's shirt. Usually that smell comforted her—not today.

Grandpa gave her another squeeze and rose to his feet. "I think maybe you just need to sit here for a while and watch for Sabrina. I'll be in the house if you need me."

"OK," Maddy whispered. But she knew she could not just wait for Sabrina; she had to *do* something. As soon as Grandpa had gone inside, she stood and began walking in circles. It felt aimless, her feet moving along in an arc with the butternut tree at its center, but somehow it soothed her. *If I don't stop, if I keep on walking, maybe I will see Nata riding out of the woods—or the meadow,* thought Maddy. So, for the rest of the morning, she went in ever-widening arcs out to the field, looping through the edge of the woods, always keeping her eyes on the ground. Once Grandpa waved to her from the open front door, and she waved back. Holding up a glass, he yelled, "Want some lemonade?"

Shaking her head, Maddy kept moving—around the back, the front, down to the line of pines that separated Grandpa's meadow from the graveyard. And all that time she thought to herself, words beating in time with the thump of her heels, *How do you get used to losing something you've never even known?*

Finally, she came to rest, sitting once again under the butternut tree. She felt empty, as if some piece had been taken out of her insides and thrown away. Staring out over the meadow grass, she saw it waving as if a breeze blew, a sinuous, running ripple that came toward her. Maddy lifted her head. The wind wasn't blowing. The ripple flowed across the field, and out of the tall grasses walked Sabrina with Nata on her back.

Bubbles rose inside of Maddy until she thought she could jump into the sky. Trying not to shout, Maddy ran toward them. "You came back! What happened?"

Nata crouched over the cat's neck, pulling his cap down under the rush of her words. Maddy saw she was frightening him and knelt on the lawn.

"What happened?" she whispered as he dismounted from Sabrina.

His face was hard and set. It seemed to have aged since she last saw him. "Sala sent me away, Madd-ee; he does not trust me anymore. He said I must perform a great deed before I can be allowed to return. And he told me I have put the whole camp in danger by talking to you. He is right!"

"No, he isn't," Maddy replied. "I won't tell anyone about you or the camp. Your secret is safe with me. Oh, Sabrina!" She reached out to touch her cat. "Oh, Sabrina," she whispered.

The cat came up to her, purring and butting her head against Maddy's hand.

"What a fine animal this is!" Nata said. "She took me

past the watchers in the wood; I rode under her belly!"

"Under her belly?" Maddy repeated.

"Yes. We have a tale about an elf child who clung to the underside of a weasel. And I thought, if a weasel, why not a cat? Then they did not see me when I went past." He patted Sabrina's shoulder.

Maddy yearned to be part of his life, to know what it was like to be so small that you could ride beneath a cat. "Oh," was all she could say, "oh."

"'Oh,' is right, Maddy. Here you are at last!" said Grandpa from a great height. "And who is this with you?" Crouching, he peered at Nata.

Nata seemed frozen, unable to run and hide. Hand still touching the cat's fur, he gasped.

"You, sirra, are something not seen before on this earth," whispered Grandpa, as if he knew loud sounds would frighten Nata.

Suddenly, Nata sprang to life. "I have been seen before on this earth!" he snapped. "*We* were here before you. We were here when there were only unicorns and eagles and never-ending grass."

Sighing, Grandpa sank to the ground. Tears came to his eyes. "Tell me more, tell me about the time of the unicorns."

"A long time ago in the green land," began Nata, and then punched his fist into one hand. "What am I doing? Talking to *another* human? Now I know I will be banished forever!" He sent out one blue-black note that hung above them, shimmering in the early afternoon light.

Grandpa reached up and touched the note. It dented in one side, gave a low, vibrating sound, and rose higher into the air. "Oh, my Lord," whispered Grandpa. "What thing is this?"

"You saw?" Nata asked. "You *saw* my sorrow call?"

Grandpa nodded. "If that is what it is. I know you are sad, whoever you are—whatever you are."

Maddy gripped his shoulder. "You can see Nata's song—just as I did. Sala told Nata that humans can *never* see the songs of elves."

"Elves!" repeated Grandpa softly, smiling. "So that is what you are."

"Nata, of the Eastern Woods Clan." He clapped his hand to his mouth, then threw his cap on the ground and spat. A scarlet flower shot into the air. "Now I am deeper in trouble! I cannot open my mouth without letting out some secret!"

Maddy was bewildered; what had Nata revealed that he shouldn't have? But Grandpa appeared to know, for he said solemnly, "Then there are other clans, Mr. Elf? That is what worries you? Don't worry; we will tell no one. Will we, Maddy?" He turned to her.

"Of course not. Besides," said Maddy, grinning, "who would believe us?"

"Who indeed?" Grandpa said. "Now, you two are having some kind of conference, I can tell. What has happened? It must be something very serious to bring an elf into human company."

Smoothing his hair back, Nata picked up his cap and set it on his head. "The Horned One is back in our woods, elder human. He is the terrible great owl who devoured my parents, and He attacked me last night and may attack our camp this very night!"

"And Sala told Nata that he must perform a brave deed, Grandpa, before he will be allowed back. They said he put the whole camp in danger by talking to me."

"But *you* are not ordinary humans," Nata said, coming closer to Grandpa and peering up into his face. "You came up on us without my hearing; you saw my song. I wonder; Madd-ee already is *aleeno,* but the scrolls speak of partners." He stopped.

"I could help!" Grandpa said so loudly that Nata ran to the other side of the thick tree trunk. "Oh, come out, I didn't mean to frighten you. I'm sorry."

Nata crept around the tree trunk and watched Grandpa warily. "Help elves? Help me to battle The Horned One?" He seemed to be sizing Grandpa up, looking from his feet to the top of his head. "You are tall, and that is useful."

Grandpa went on in a softer voice. "I could bring a weapon—something to stab the owl with," he said, jabbing at the air.

"That might work," Nata said, smiling at last. "The

trouble is that our arrows bounce off His feathers—they do not have the magic to pierce His heart, all because of that long-ago elf who killed an owl."

Grandpa turned to Maddy, raising his eyebrows. She shrugged and looked at Nata.

"A vow broken," Nata explained, "all for the sake of love. And ever since, owls do not obey us, because this elf did not follow the covenant with the birds of the air. Covenant," he mused. "I wonder?"

"We could help, really we could, Nata," Maddy said eagerly. "You said yourself that we are *aleeno.*"

"Let us be more than that," Grandpa put in. "Let us be with you to battle this owl. We can be your partners, the way humans were with elves long ago."

Nata eyed them warily, twisted his hands together, and said, "I cannot take such a step until I know more of you. Here. Let us see if you can really *see.*"

Opening his mouth, Nata sent out a soft line of song. The first note plucked like a harp and was orange, the second rang like a bell and was pale yellow, the third whistled like a dove and was green, and the next sounds came with colors ranging through the blues to purple. As the song soared up, birds came to sit in the butternut, catching some of the notes in their beaks and gulping them down. First came a blue jay, raucous and swift. The song rose higher. Then a brood of wrens fluttered into the leaves, settling like soft brown buttons against the green. A little one grabbed a yellow note and chewed on it. The song went higher still, the top notes pale silver like shards of ice falling from the sky. A hawk dove down from the clouds and landed, feet outstretched. Opening his beak, he glared at them out of yellow eyes.

"Oh, Maddy!" exclaimed Grandpa, holding out his hands as if he, too, could catch the elf's notes.

Maddy could not speak; she felt silver rushing through her veins, rising up to meet the notes spiraling through the air. Opening her mouth, she sent out one shining note that lifted into the sky.

Nata turned and looked at her, closing his mouth with a sudden snap. The song stopped, and all the colored notes that were left began to fall from the sky. One settled on Grandpa's face, working its way into his ear; another flew down into the meadow grass and disappeared. Other notes gathered speed, tumbling over and under one another like strange, colored tumbleweeds. They spun off into the meadow and disappeared. Only the excited chattering of birds and animals marked their passage. And, as if a con-ductor had waved a baton, in one single movement all the birds in the tree flew into the air and swept off on the wind.

"You, human child, *that* was an elf note you sent out." Nata bowed before her and took part of her hand in his. She shivered; the touch was light and feathery, like a moth's wing. "*Now* we are partners, my family and yours, whatever happens." He bowed to Grandpa, and solemnly, Grandpa bowed in return.

"We must help you soon, Nata, before the owl returns. Couldn't we all go back to your camp and fight the owl? Then your leader would see how brave you are."

"But the watchers in the forest wouldn't let us through," Maddy interrupted.

"I wasn't finished yet," said Grandpa with great dignity. "If the owl attacks your camp tonight, everyone will be too busy to notice us. Wouldn't your outposts be called home to battle the owl?"

"They would," Nata agreed. He smiled, and a golden light settled on Maddy's and Grandpa's faces. "I have been learning Far Seeing, and my hearing is very sharp. I think I could see if the owl came tonight, or at least, could hear the hunting cry of the owl from far away."

"Then let's go!" Grandpa strode toward the house, with Maddy following.

Nata called out, "I will wait here with my cat until you are ready."

CHAPTER TWENTY

Maddy held Grandpa's hand as they went across the lawn toward the house. She could feel, with some sixth sense, Nata standing and waiting with Sabrina. *I will never get her back, never,* she thought sadly. Her mind felt scumbled and tired, as if a wind had blown things inside. Birds eating song. Colored notes soaring to the sky. One rolling into Grandpa's ear.

She had a sudden, sharp insight; magic wasn't all wonder and joy. It was a wind that picked you up and set you down someplace new and strange; it was the tiredness after the wind had passed. It was feeling as if your insides had been scrambled. Her hair hurt, as if someone had been pulling it. When they stopped on the kitchen step, Maddy leaned against Grandpa.

Gently, he rubbed her back. "It's a bit much, isn't it, pumpkin? Are you feeling a little tired? I am! This is a lot to take in at one time." He grinned at her, and they went into the house together. "Don't you think we should take some sleeping bags with us? Then we can camp out while we're waiting to see if the owl will attack."

"OK, Grandpa." *Will it be all right? Will we be safe?* she wondered. Up the stairs to the attic they went, looking for Grandpa's old sleeping bags.

Maddy felt a sense of urgency and almost shouted at Grandpa to hurry as he bent over some bundles, searching for the bags. She poked and prodded, only finding boxes of books that smelled musty and an old dollhouse with its top floor broken.

"Here they are, here they are!" crowed Grandpa, holding up two yellowing sleeping bags.

Sneezing, they dragged the sleeping bags downstairs and beat the dust out of them over the railings by the kitchen steps. They sneezed again and again as big clouds of dust puffed up and were blown away.

"These haven't been used in a while, Maddy, not since your mother was a little girl. She had them at that camp she loved, Camp Windigo, I think it was. Everything was so ordered there, not like home! Your mother has always loved order."

He rolled up the sleeping bags, tied them with cords, and went back inside. "Here, Maddy," he said, holding out a knapsack. "You stuff in some of these granola bars, sandwiches, those puddings we like, and juice cans. What does the elf eat?"

"Nata, Grandpa, his name is Nata."

"Well, Nata, then. What does he eat? Fireflies and dew?" He chuckled.

"No! Berries, water, vegetables, things like that."

"Then tuck in some carrots and grapes for him, Maddy, and let's go." Grandpa tied one of the sleeping bags to the backpack, shrugged it on his shoulders, and gave the other one to Maddy. "You'll have to carry that, honey. Come on."

"Wait a minute." She pulled on his arm. "What about a weapon, Grandpa, something to use against the great horned owl?"

"Ah, yes. I thought of that." He held out a tent pole he'd found in the attic and thrust it forward. "There, just like a sword. It's got a pretty sharp point."

His eyes gleamed as he hummed to himself. *How can he be happy?* she wondered. She felt nervous, itchy, and wished it were all over. Tying a sweater around her waist—it might be cold at night in the woods—Maddy shouldered the sleeping bag and followed Grandpa out the door.

Maddy felt a slight jolt inside as she saw Nata waiting beside *her* cat. Nata waved at them, pushed his cap up, and jumped onto the cat. Gripping the reins firmly, he said, "Come with me." They walked through the meadow, across the street, and into the shadowy edges of the wood.

"I didn't know you could go this way," Grandpa said as they followed Nata downhill through the trees. They walked for a long time, and Maddy saw that Sabrina was flagging. She realized the cat had made this journey twice today, and her heart ached for Sabrina.

"Not so fast!" she wanted to shout to Nata. "Be careful of her!" But Maddy did not say anything, afraid that the elf would just race off on his own.

Though it was hard going, they finally pushed through the trees to the familiar dirt road, and Nata rode Sabrina over the bridge, into the shelter of the forest. Sounds faded until all they heard was birdsong and the faint rustle of a nearby stream.

"I'm tired," Maddy whispered to Grandpa, who took her hand in his.

It was some time later that Nata finally stopped by a large pine, dismounted, and rubbed Sabrina's fur with a soft piece of leather. After feeding her some red berries, he held up his hand. "We must talk softly," he whispered, "so the watchers in the wood will not hear us. No sudden noises, please, no loud words."

Grandpa nodded and surveyed the ground. Carefully, he bent over some saplings and brush to clear a place for the sleeping bags Maddy was unrolling. Nata set up his own camp nearby, gathering a pile of soft moss. Grandpa unpacked some food and began to eat.

"Maddy?" he said, holding out a sandwich. "Nata, some grapes?"

Delicately, Nata took a grape and nibbled at it. Grandpa smiled. "Pudding?" he offered.

"Pud-ding?" Nata tested the word. "What is that?"

"Try it," Maddy said.

Nata gripped the spoon as if it were a sword and tasted a little from the edge. He spat it out on the ground. "Pugh! I do not like pudding! Now," he said, waving his hand at them. "Please do not talk for a while, and I will try what I know of Far Seeing."

He sat on his bed of moss, eyes closed so tightly that wrinkles laced his skin. He breathed slightly, his chest barely rising and falling. His skin paled silver, and beads of moisture appeared.

He sighed, then groaned. "It is hard to see—I know so little yet. But I think the owl is getting ready to hunt. I see Him shaking out His feathers and opening His beak. I think He will hunt elves tonight!" Nata opened his eyes.

"Then we will be there to get Him!" Grandpa shook his spear.

Maddy wondered what she could do to help. Hold up a sharp stick? Yell and scream? Nervously, she hoped she'd know when the time came; she was Nata's partner and must not fail him.

"How close are we to your camp, Nata?" Maddy asked as the last yellow light touched the trees.

"Not too far, Madd-ee. When the owl attacks, He will give His hunting cry, and I will hear it."

And what will I do? Maddy wondered. *Run? Stand by and do nothing?* Worrying, she watched the sky turn pink, then red. After a time it changed to a pale green that seemed to shine within itself. The green slid down into the dark needles of the pines. To Maddy, it seemed as if the dark rose from the thick branches of the trees, blotting out all light. The forest was ominous, dense, impenetrable. Shivering, Maddy put her legs into her sleeping bag and pulled it up to her chin.

Nata sat, staring into the darkness. With his cap off, his hair stood out around his face in a silver halo, sending a faint light to the forest floor. *He is afraid, too,* Maddy thought, *just like me.*

The only one who didn't seem frightened was Grandpa. Humming softly to himself, he eased into his sleeping bag and lay down, head on his folded arms. As suddenly as a small child, he slept. Maddy kept her eyes open, watching the stars overhead. She could not close her eyes, afraid that something might creep up on her while she was sleeping.

But she must have slept, briefly, for suddenly Nata was by her ear, whispering, "He's coming. Hurry! I hear His hunting cry."

Maddy jumped up, pulled on her sweater, and shook Grandpa awake. He was on his feet in an instant, grabbing his spear as Nata mounted Sabrina. Maddy was surprised at how swiftly they went through the woods. Branches seemed to part before them, and the brush bent to the ground.

The air was heavy and cool. Sounds came to Maddy, faraway shouts and cries. They ran faster, keeping Nata and Sabrina just in sight. Suddenly, they were at the edge of a large clearing where small creatures moved in and out of flickering shadows and the light from a big bonfire. With a hasty glance, Maddy saw some kind of bark lodges at the edge of the clearing.

Dismounting, Nata leapt forward. He ran to the side of other elves who were aiming their bows upward. At a signal, they loosed their arrows into the sky. Something whooshed overhead, turned, and came back again. An elf yelled, pointing at Maddy and Grandpa, but the rest of the camp were too busy to notice.

"Owls!" Maddy seized Grandpa's arm. "*Two* of them!"

Grandpa ran into the clearing, spear held high. Maddy

grabbed a stick from the underbrush and followed, heart thumping. She was afraid, but if she was going to help Nata, this was the time.

Suddenly, the owls were upon them. Wings gliding soundlessly and talons out, they swept down upon the camp.

CHAPTER TWENTY-ONE

Nata saw The Horned One flying over camp, His dark wings shadowing the elves. Shrieks of fright came from the bark lodges as the owl turned soundlessly and swept down. He raked one of the birch-bark dwellings, and elves dove for cover in the near bushes. At the same time, another hunting cry tore across the clearing.

One group of armed elves raised their bows toward The Horned One and loosed their arrows as another group faced His mate. Helplessly, the elves watched their arrows bounce off the first bird's feathers. He dove toward an escaping elf child and grabbed her in His left talon. Crying out His triumph, He flew to a pine, landing soundlessly.

His mate circled the camp, escaping the arrows, then turned and dove toward an elf near Maddy. All she could see were the fierce talons. "Grandpa!" Maddy yelled, jumping toward the owl. The bird rocked to the side, raked upward, and swung around again as the elf fled for cover.

As Nata saw The Horned One settling in the tall pine, the cries of the youngling reached his ears. Rage filled Nata, and he seemed to swell and lighten with a red heat inside. Running for the pine, he saw three others beside him as they swarmed up the trunk, digging their clawed sixth fingers into the bark. Up, up they went, with the sound of the owl's triumph ringing above.

When Nata's head poked above the top branches, he saw the great owl bending over the youngling. Anger raced through his body, lifting him into the air, up under the owl's wings. Nata jabbed at the belly, dagger going in to the hilt. The Horned One screamed and rose into the air as blood burned Nata's face. Crying out, he saw Cala catch the elf child as she fell. Then Nata dropped to the branch below.

The Horned One thumped His wings together like some dark wind gathering itself. He flew out above the tree, shrieking. Images flooded Nata's mind: his mother gripped by the owl's talons, her screams rising with His. As in a dream, Nata saw his father racing along the ground but never catching up. Rage sang in Nata's veins, and he shot into the air again. This time the anger propelled him through the sky toward the dark, flapping shape.

"Go for the eyes, Nata, the eyes!" yelled Grandpa from below. "The feathers are too thick!"

As Nata came nearer, the owl screamed and beat His wings against Nata's face and head. Nata faltered and dropped back. He saw the yellow eyes above, and lower, the outstretched talons. Maddy shrieked, and he heard Hele call out. Red-hot anger surged through Nata as he rose above the owl, swooped, and stabbed His eye. With a wild cry, the owl began to fall, but one talon grabbed Nata. Pain pierced Nata's side, the sky rushed past, and darkness slammed up to meet him.

CHAPTER TWENTY-TWO

"Nata!" Maddy raced toward the fallen bird. Grandpa turned the great horned owl over with his spear, showing the dark, sprawled shape of the elf still gripped in one talon. Raising his metal pole, Grandpa stabbed the owl again and again.

"Must . . . make . . . sure . . . he's . . . dead," he grunted. Blood covered the end of his pole. Maddy stared at Grandpa. He seemed like some wild, fierce warrior, not at all like her grandpa.

The wings twitched and then stilled forever as the talons unclenched, and Nata slipped to the ground. Above, they heard the dreadful cry of the owl's mate as She circled over camp. Then She turned and disappeared over the trees.

A crowd gathered around the dead owl and Grandpa and Maddy. Small twitterings and low voices sounded. An elf woman with silver hair raced up and knelt beside Nata. Calling out strange words, she and two others lifted Nata and carried him to a bark dwelling. When Maddy went and crouched by the low doorway, the woman held out her arms in a forbidding gesture.

"No!" The words were halting. "You . . . must go."

But Maddy heard other words from the group: "Humans . . . helped . . . like olden times; they are *aleeno,* friends."

An elf with a lined face came out of the circle, stood before Grandpa, and spoke fluently. "You must have learned of our camp from Nata. We are grateful to you for aiding us, but you must go home. It is dangerous for elves to talk with humans. We will have to leave, now that you know where we live."

"But we will never bother you." Maddy stepped forward. The older elf backed away, holding up hands that glowed in the darkness. A silver light shone on Maddy, circling her head. Suddenly, all she wanted was to go home and sleep. The elves faded, her worry about Nata disappeared; all she saw was her four-poster bed at Grandpa's house.

Grandpa took Maddy's hand, leading her away from the clearing. "Nata will be all right," he whispered. "Don't worry."

When they ducked under the trees, Grandpa knelt and picked up something from the ground. "My flashlight. I thought I might need this." He waved it at Maddy and turned it on. Warm yellow light flowed ahead of them, lighting their way.

Even though Maddy yearned for her bed, something made her turn and look back; a faint red from the bonfire showed through the trees. She heard a low murmuring sound, then rising voices. The elves seemed to be chanting, and she wondered what they were going to do with the owl. *But they don't want us,* Maddy thought. *We have to go home, and I'll never see Nata again. And never see Sabrina, either.*

Maddy slipped her hand into Grandpa's. He looked down at her. "Tired, pumpkin? You were my brave girl, going after that other owl with your stick. I'm proud of you!" He hugged her shoulder and began to whistle tunelessly.

"Grandpa! How can you whistle at a time like this?"

"Why not at a time like this? Didn't we help the elves?

Didn't we help protect them? How many humans could say that!" She could see his grin in the moonlight.

They reached the place where they had camped. To Maddy, it seemed that days had passed since they lay there beside Nata.

"No sense in staying here tonight, Maddy," Grandpa said, bending and rolling up their sleeping bags. He packed what was left of their supper into the knapsack and slipped his arms into the straps.

"But, Grandpa, we can't just go." Maddy tugged on his arm. "What if that other owl comes back? Maybe the elves will need us again."

"They won't let us enter camp," Grandpa said. "They would find some way to keep us out." He stretched and yawned. "Strange, but all I can think about is bed."

"Grandpa? Do you think Nata's brave deed will be what he needed?"

Grandpa nodded, shouldering his sleeping bag. "Killing The Horned One must count. That band isn't so big that they can afford to let Nata go." He took her hand. "Come on."

They walked slowly through the moonlit forest, and tears slid down Maddy's cheeks. She *had* helped, she really had! Nata was grateful to them, she knew, but it wasn't enough. There were still things to do; she had never given Nata back his saddle, and *he* had never given her her true name. Whatever it was.

Grandpa did not say anything else on the way home. When they went through the kitchen door, he dropped their sleeping bags in the middle of the room and yawned.

"I'm off to bed, pumpkin. Try to get some sleep. We'll talk about it in the morning." Giving her a warm hug, he patted her on the back. Feet dragging, Maddy climbed the stairs to her room and curled up in bed without taking her clothes off. The empty space next to her pillow seemed filled with darkness, and Maddy rubbed her eyes fiercely. *I have lost two things this night—my elf and my cat.*

Chapter Twenty-Three

Nata swam in red heat. Wings beat about his head. Blood dripped on his face and seared his skin. He could hear the cries of his companions, and the frightened whimpers of the child. Again and again, he rose into the air, dagger in hand. Over and over, he plunged it into the owl's eye.

"Hush, hush," a voice soothed. A song coiled out around his head.

———

Darkness flee from elf,
fear pass from wound,
heal up, bind up skin.

Something pierced his skin, a small series of pricks that accompanied the song. He felt the edges of his wound draw together, and the awful spilling out of *hislin* stopped. Warmth penetrated him, and he opened his eyes.

Hele was holding a cup of hot broth to his lips. "Hush, drink, don't try to talk." Behind her he thought he saw other faces, but shadows covered them. Sounds came to him—roaring into his ears, then receding into the distance. Out of the rush of sound a few words were clear: "Master destroyer—rage flier—killer of The Horned One."

He tried to sit up, but Hele gently pushed him back against the bed. "Don't move. You have been gravely wounded by the owl. We are singing your skin together."

Dimly, he was aware of Lele sitting near him. She joined her voice to Hele's, and the songs wove over and under each other, silver notes darting along the edges of his wound. Then his side glowed a healthy pink, and the dreadful darkness of the wound began to pass away.

"There, better now," someone breathed. "Sleep, Nata, sleep."

He dove into a dreamless state and did not rise to the surface again until the next day. When he sat up in bed,

Hele was there, with warm *lelan* on a plate and a cup of partridgeberry tea.

"Here, this will help."

He chewed on the bread, made from the golden pollen of cattails, and felt its warmth fill him. The tea flowed down inside, taking away some of last night's shadows.

"The Horned One?" he finally asked. "What happened to Him?"

"You killed Him," Hele said proudly. "You rose up in your anger and stabbed His eye."

"That is what the elder human told me to do," Nata said. "He and Madd-ee helped me, Hele."

"I know." She smoothed the blanket up to his chin. "And then—" She stopped.

"Then what? All I remember is falling and darkness."

"Because that is what happened. He took you with Him when He fell, wrapping you about with His death. We almost lost you, Nata." She took his hand and held it to her cheek. "Lele had to go to the House of Scrolls and search through them for the strongest healing songs. But they worked!"

Nata tried to smile but could not. Still, he felt wrapped in pain, just as the owl's wings had enfolded him. He put a hand up to touch his cheek and felt ridged skin.

"Shhh, it will heal in time." Hele stroked his cheek. "Now, here is someone to see you. Not too long, Sala, he is still weak," she said, standing and making room.

Sala came and stood by his bed. "You are better, now, Nata?" he asked, face creased with worry lines.

"Yes, I am better. I still hurt, though."

"I should think so. Flying into the air in your rage and stabbing The Horned One's eye! Even now, the bards are making songs about it. This will last long in our history. It is time to give you your inner name. As soon as you are well, we will have the naming ceremony."

Nata started. Usually elves did not get a second name until they were one hundred years old.

"Then"—he frowned and winced—"you trust me again?"

Sala smiled. "Of course! Your brave act has canceled out what happened with the humans—more than canceled out!"

Nata let his head sink back against the cattail pillow. All of his joints ached from that terrible fall, but a thread of song started up inside. He was home. *Home.*

Then he mouthed the words, "What of the other owl?" His lips dried, and Hele came forward with more tea.

"That one is still abroad," Sala said grimly. "And She will come back, I'm certain. But that is not for you to worry about now. You must get well first."

"Sala, what of the humans? Madd-ee and her grandfather helped us."

"I know, but I had to send them away. I had to!" he repeated as Nata frowned. "They were a danger to us all.

The younglings wanted to touch them and talk with them. Soon all humans for miles around would know where we live. As soon as you are well enough to travel, we must leave."

"They would not betray us. They fed me and gave me shelter. And"—he passed his hand over his face, remembering—"both heard and saw my songs, Sala."

"What?" The older elf started forward. "That cannot be! No human has ever *seen* an elf song, maybe heard it in the old, green days, but never saw one."

"Madd-ee and her grandfather did."

The two elves were silent for a moment, thinking different thoughts. Nata missed Madd-ee, her bright chatter, her joy at knowing him. And he missed the wise face of the old one.

"I know you wish this would change everything, but it cannot," Sala finally said. "We still must keep our distance from people. In silence is safety, in blind humans is our salvation."

"Maybe," said Nata, "but not this time. Madd-ee and her grandfather helped us, and we may need them again."

A dreadful tiredness seized Nata. Turning his head on the pillow, he heard Hele murmuring to Sala. The door opened and closed, a fresh breath of air wafting over him. As he closed his eyes, he thought, *I must see Madd-ee again, for she promised to return my saddle, and I promised her her true name.*

CHAPTER TWENTY-FOUR

Maddy woke and stretched. Her hand touched the cold hollow that Sabrina should have occupied. Sadness welled up inside. Again she felt like that picture on Grandpa's wall, where Adam and Eve had to flee paradise. *My cat. My elf.* She had had a glimpse of something so wonderful that she could not bear to be without it. Pulling Grandma's sunflower quilt up to her chin, Maddy closed her eyes. *How can I ever live a normal life again, now that I've known an elf?*

Slowly she put her bare feet on the floor and dressed

in ragged jeans and an old T-shirt. Downstairs, Grandpa was sitting at the kitchen table, sipping black coffee from his blue mug. In between sips, he hummed.

Maddy sat down at the table and planted her elbows. "Grandpa, how can you sing? Look at what we've lost! We had an elf living in our tree house!"

"We never *had* an elf, Maddy. You can't 'have' an elf. I rather think it's the other way around."

"But he said we were partners, Grandpa. Doesn't that mean something?" Maddy asked. She held up two fingers twisted around each other, the way she remembered Nata doing. Catching her breath, she missed him so much that her chest felt hollow.

Suddenly, Maddy reached out and took a piece of paper and a pen from the pile on the table. "I'm going to write down everything I can remember that Nata said. Then maybe, maybe . . ." She blinked her eyes rapidly.

Grandpa smoothed her hair. "Then maybe he won't seem so far away, pumpkin. Good idea. I wish I could write down the notes to his song, the one where the birds came and perched in the tree, and all the colors of the world went up into the sky. Then"—he sighed—"then the colors rolled off into the meadow. Can you believe it was just yesterday, Maddy?"

"Grandpa! Your eyes!"

He put his hand up. "What about them?"

"They just turned turquoise, Grandpa."

"Ah," he sighed. "Then some of the elves' magic is left in us. I feel it, don't you?"

Maddy nodded, then rose quickly, abandoning the pen and paper. "Maybe the notes Nata sang are still in the meadow. I'm going to look."

"Maddy?" Grandpa called after her, but she was gone, racing across the mowed lawn to the edge of the field. There the colored notes had spun out of sight between the tall grasses, the black-eyed Susans, and the whispery dry stalks.

Crouching, Maddy began to go through the meadow, pulling the grasses gently aside. She saw a cricket clutching a stem and heard its frightened cry. To her left was a grass nest hiding inside a thick bush. Nearby, a shred of orange was caught on a briar. It fluttered in the breeze, and from it rose a sweet, tangerine scent. It reminded Maddy of the Christmas tangerine that always rested in the toe of her stocking. Without thinking, she took the small flag of orange from the bush and held it to her nose. It vibrated gently against her skin. She smelled it and then opened her mouth, popping it inside as if it were candy. *Didn't the birds eat the notes of Nata's song? Why can't I, then?*

Maddy swallowed. Her throat felt warm, and heat flowed down to her stomach. She opened her mouth and sang. There were no words, just a sweet, wild melody that soared up. Then she felt the meadow shift under her, and all the songs of the meadow chirped against her ear.

Near her foot came the twitterings of a new litter of mice.

>My place, mine
>my turn, mine

they chattered as they struggled to nurse at their mother's belly. She could feel the heat from their new bodies rising up through the nest.

Sitting quietly for a moment, Maddy felt the feathered grass sweep against her skin in the warm breeze. Something burrowed through the soil underneath; small vibrations itched under her seat, and a star-shaped snout thrust out of the earth. It rotated around, and a soft, plush head peered over a mound of dirt.

>Worms?
>Any worms?
>Or a dead beetle,
>and a worm, a worm!

Maddy grinned. The star-nosed mole drew its head back into its tunnel and worked under the soil again. Suddenly, a shadow passed overhead, and she ducked, heart pounding. All she could think of was the owl, with talons outstretched. Little animals scurried into their burrows, and Maddy heard their frightened cries.

Red-tail, red-tail,
find us not!
Sharp mouth, sharp claw,
go elsewhere!

The shadow swept over the meadow, and Maddy saw the hawk soaring above a line of trees. As it disappeared, she heard its disconsolate cry.

Woe is me,
no food today,
empty belly,
woe is me!

Maddy shivered. Words fell out of the sky. Sunlight ran down her arms like golden water. She shook her hands, and drops of sunlight scattered on the ground. Maddy jumped, and her nose filled with meadow scents. Grass had a warm, milky smell; the earth beneath was rich and meaty; nearby were mice smelling like fusty dogs; and the crickets had a dry, almost lemony scent.

Maddy didn't know if she was going to laugh or cry. *So many new things all at once. How can I ever be the same?* Maybe she felt the way Daddy did after playing a long, passionate piece of music. Afterward, he said, he was drained, as if he had poured out the notes from inside.

Unsteadily, watching where she put her feet, Maddy rose. Songs and smells fluttered up from the ground as she waded back through the field to tell Grandpa.

CHAPTER TWENTY-FIVE

Maddy paused on the top front step, arms across her chest. Hearing all the songs of the meadow made her think of Nata. The orange note had filled her with happiness, but there was a tinge of sadness. Where was Nata now? She *wished* she had remembered to give him that saddle. Was he healed? He'd said that *hislin* healed all wounds, but that owl had given Nata a vicious, deep rake with His claws.

Watching a crow take wing, Maddy heard its hoarse voice.

145

Hungry, nothing to eat,
bare field, pah!

If she could understand birds talking, what would she hear if she had her true name from Nata? He had said names were important, and she imagined *something* would happen if she had an elf name. *It will never happen now,* she thought. *I will never know.* Shivering, she went inside and sat close beside Grandpa at the kitchen table.

There was so much to tell that she could not begin. He put down his pen and ruffled her hair.

"Did you find any of Nata's colored notes?"

"One," she answered, smiling. "One orange one. I think orange is for happiness, for it made me happy. And I could hear"—she opened her hand—"oh, such things!"

"Tell me." He rested his chin in his hands.

"There was the song of the hawk—he was very crabby because he couldn't find anything to eat. And the small animals of the field shrieked and chattered when he passed over. They sang out words for him to leave them alone."

"And did he?"

"Mmm, he did fly off. But before that a mole poked its head up right by me and asked for worms, or a beetle." She laughed, remembering. "And I could understand what the baby mice were saying. They were fighting over their mother's milk."

"You could understand that?"

"Yes, and I felt like Alice in Wonderland when she ate the wrong side of the mushroom. Huge." They grinned at each other. "And strange, Grandpa," Maddy added.

"I know, pumpkin." He patted her hand. "I've been hearing things, too."

"You have?" Maddy was almost jealous. She thought *she* was the only one.

"The mice were in the walls last night, having a rugby game. Some of them were chattering and cheering, Maddy. I hardly slept a wink. It was like a party!

"And then," Grandpa went on, "before you were up, I saw the skunk that lives under my barn. She had five young skunks following—all bright eyes and white, bushy tails. They looked like little rugs!"

Maddy laughed. "Did they say anything?"

"They grumbled. 'Don't get too close,' 'Watch out,' 'Hurry up!' and 'Leave some grubs for me.'"

They sat for a moment, shoulders touching.

"We'll never be the same again, Grandpa," Maddy said. "I don't know if that's a good or a bad thing. I already felt different before. Now I'm going to be even *more* unusual."

"Well, as you say, you already were different. Do you think it will be that much of a change?" Grandpa encircled her with his arm.

Maddy took in the scent of Grandpa's shirt: warm, comforting, with a faint odor of soap. "What if I'm walking through the park with a friend, and suddenly I hear the squirrels talking? How can I act normal if that happens?"

He smiled down at her. "You'll have to be two people, Maddy, an inside person and an outside person."

Maddy sat for a moment, thinking. Then she nodded. "I guess that's what I'll have to be. But I don't like it."

Grandpa stopped smiling. "Well, Maddy, gifts mean problems; they don't mean easy times."

Maddy thought of her parents, of Father's gift and Mother's. They could make their fingers fly over the keys and make sounds that moved people. Daddy said that he had been born with music in his fingertips, and that he didn't always like that. Maybe he had wanted to be normal, too—to teach or work in an office like her friend Emily's father.

"I don't know." She sighed, and suddenly her eyes filled with tears. "I just wish I could see Nata once more and say good-bye. And I wish, I just *wish* I had Sabrina back!"

"Don't you wish for something else?" Grandpa said in an odd tone. "Remember that before Nata made us part-ners with him, I could see and understand him. I'd like to know why you and I can hear the elves and other people can't. What makes *us* special, Maddy?"

She looked at him, rubbing her finger down the back of his hand. Did she imagine it, or was there a faint silver glow to his skin? "I don't know, Grandpa. I never got a chance to find out!"

CHAPTER TWENTY-SIX

"Stay here."

"I cannot sit by while the whole camp works." Nata stood up.

"You are not healed yet," Hele said, pushing him gently back down on the bed. "Even Sala and Lele said to rest. We have only waited this long to give you time to knit together. And we must be gone before the humans come back—or the owl's mate."

As Hele packed all her goods in deerskin bags, cinching the tops, Nata fumed. Her bow and arrows were laid on top of the two bundles. She traveled light, as did everyone in camp. The only possessions they had were a few changes of clothes, some cooking pots, and their precious scrolls.

"I must do *something!*" He rose and went to the open doorway. Children danced around the dying bonfire where they had burned the great owl two nights ago. One child took up a stick and rushed at the embers, shouting and screaming. Another boy thrust a stick at the sky, scowling fiercely as the children yelled at an imaginary attacker.

Nata smiled. So little and so fierce. In time they would be warriors, if need be, and tellers of tales, ones who guarded the woods and forests.

Sala strode into the clearing as the last rays touched Nata's face. Their leader had told them they would leave this night, even though the owl might still be near. For elves always made their journeys in darkness, even in long-ago times.

"Ready?" Hele asked behind him.

Nata started and nodded silently. Just outside the door waited his cat and Hele's, brought there by Cala. Nata went to his mount and stroked her ears, wishing he had gotten his saddle back from Madd-ee, but it was not to be. He glanced around the camp.

All of the mounts were lined up in a row with their owners beside them, gripping the animals' bridles. Some cats were laden with sacks of goods; two had small carts attached to a special harness around their middle.

"Our scrolls," Hele whispered beside him. "I hope they will be safe."

"Of course they will," Nata answered. The baskets containing the scrolls were firmly lashed to the sides of the carts.

Lele stood in the clearing and blew on a silver trumpet. The mounts skittered at the sound and were only calmed when their owners sang songs into their ears. Sala stood beside Lele, dressed in his journeying clothes. Special designs coiled around the hem of his tunic and down its sleeves, designs for protection on the journey, and for luck.

Sala spoke. "It is time to go, elves of the Eastern Woods Clan; time to leave this beautiful forest where we have lived for so long. We have seen new ones born here, elves joined for life, tales told, songs sung. Part of our history has been sung into the bark of this forest. But it is time to move on. Even if it weren't for the attacks of the owls, we would have to leave, for we have been seen by *laglan.* It is only a matter of time before another human discovers us and tries to use us in some way."

There was a murmuring response, and Lele added, "Tread lightly, walk swiftly, and we will head for the cold country. Fewer people live there, and we can build new lodges deep in the woods, away from voices and roads."

"But what about new mounts, Sala?" asked a younger elf.

"We will make a special foray to find new ones when needed," Sala answered in a clipped voice.

Then Lele sang a lilting tune that circled them, lightly touching the head of each elf. A faint, gleaming thread went from one to another, all the way around the clearing. Sighing, Nata pressed a hand to his chest, happy that he was no longer alone. Stiffly, he swung his leg over his cat and watched Hele jump onto the back of her mount nearby.

Lele blew another note on her trumpet, and the elves began to move; some rode their cats, others walked behind holding their children and goods. The pack animals brought up the rear, with the carts at the very end.

Suddenly, a scream tore through the dusk. A child shrieked. A cat yowled and bolted for the underbrush. Flying out of the night sky came The Horned One's mate, wings outspread, beak open. Heat rushed out of it and a rank, choking smell. The owl screamed again, and the cry tore through the band, scattering them to the sides of the path. Elves hid in the shadows, pulling their bowstrings taut.

Jumping off his cat, Nata braced his back against a sapling. Fitting a shaft to the bowstring, he saw Hele kneeling beside him, her bow and arrow at the ready. The owl turned and swept downward again. Closer, closer, talons out, ready to rake the gathering. Nata and Hele loosed their arrows at the same time. The arrows sped toward the owl, bounced off Her claw, and She faltered.

A volley of arrows followed. *Twack! Thunk! Shhh-mmmm!* They probed the darkness, seeking the owl's soft, vulnerable belly. But She had been well taught by Her mate, and She landed in a thick pine, surveying the elves below.

Nata could see the gleam of one yellow eye through the branches. An eye like that had picked out his mother and father long ago. An eye like that had chosen him for death. He rushed toward the pine and began to climb, digging the claw on his sixth finger into the bark. Other elves swarmed up beside him. Just as they approached the feathered belly of the owl, She swept off into the air again. She was gone before Nata could nock an arrow and send it flying. Someone called out an ancient song of death, and Nata realized it was Hele singing nearby. He looked down to see her braced against the tree trunk, arrow aimed upward.

"She'll come back," Cala called out. "She is hungry and stupid with Her hunger. We will wait here."

Breathless in the warm, dusky air, bones still aching from the last fight, Nata waited as the light sank into the forest.

CHAPTER TWENTY-SEVEN

A little before sunset, Maddy sat under the butternut tree. The tree house looked hollow and empty. There was no song spilling from overhead. There was no small, sharp face to question and talk with her. Maddy put her hand to her chest and pressed in. *Something.* Something was wrong. With her new sixth sense, the back of her neck prickled and goose bumps ran up her arms. There was a sudden awareness of danger winging in. Blackness moved behind her eyelids, and a long, faint scream sounded. Shuddering, she rose and ran inside the house.

1 5 4

"Grandpa?"

He looked up from the book he was reading. "What, pumpkin? You look in a hurry."

"I think something's wrong with Nata, Grandpa." She twisted her hands together.

Grandpa sighed. "You're sure?"

"I'm sure, Grandpa."

Setting his book aside, he asked, "What do you want to do, then?"

"Go back there—through the woods. See if we can find and help the elves."

"But, pumpkin, we *can't* go back. They were very clear about that the last time. They don't want us, and we couldn't get by the watchers anyway."

"Please, Grandpa, I won't be able to sleep knowing they might need us. Please!" She jigged at his side, holding his arm.

He looked at her, smiled, and said, "Oh, all right! Maybe we won't be able to find them, but let's try. I'll bring my spear again."

"And I'm getting that saddle of Nata's," Maddy said, running upstairs for it. She put it in her knapsack along with a flashlight and a paring knife. She was afraid to use the knife, but afraid to be without it. Grandpa drove them down the hill toward the ice-cream stand. Turning onto the road, this time he did not stop but drove the car carefully down the winding dirt road. Over the bridge they went, only stopping when they reached the tall oak. He and Maddy jumped out.

They set off through the tall, wet grass toward the woods. Grass slapped their legs, and then they were in the aspen grove. Pulling branches away from their faces, they went over the wet moss and leaves.

The light changed as they went deeper into the forest. The sun sank in the sky, and birds gathered overhead, settling into the trees. Maddy heard birdsong this time, but not words. It worried her. Did that mean the elves had already left, and she and Grandpa would come to an empty clearing?

After some time they stopped to rest on the bank of a stream. Grandpa knelt and drank deeply, as did Maddy.

"Aren't we getting nearer? This looks a little familiar, Maddy. Isn't that the big pine where we camped with Nata?"

Maddy nodded, and they moved at a faster pace. It would not be long now.

Suddenly, Maddy heard a noise ahead. Her heart lifted as she saw small, flickering lights; maybe they weren't too late to help. Then came shouts, screams, and—raising gooseflesh along her arms—the long, unearthly call of an owl.

Maddy and Grandpa burst into the clearing, and Maddy saw small figures running around its edges. Some elves were kneeling, bows in hand. Arrows shot into the sky.

Maddy looked up. The huge owl was plummeting to the ground, heading for a white-haired elf standing alone, with raised spear. As he jabbed upward, the owl slipped sideways, then landed, seizing him in Her claws. She didn't fly with him, but ripped and tore at his clothes. Elves circled the predator, shooting arrows that bounced harmlessly off Her thick feathers.

As the white-haired elf struggled in the owl's talons, suddenly he cried out and opened his arms. Some elves jumped on the creature's back, trying to stab through the feathers. Maddy saw Nata rushing across the ground. Without thinking, Maddy pulled out her knife and raced forward. She stabbed the owl's neck, and blood spurted over her hand and over the elves beside her. Some cried out and jumped away. Singing a wild song, a female elf thrust her dagger into the owl up to the hilt, and the owl flapped Her wings once, twice, and fell on Her side, beside the fallen white-haired elf.

One elf with long silver hair rushed up to the figure on the ground. "Sala, Sala!" she shrieked. Cupping his face in her hands, she knelt beside him.

"He's dead." She turned to Maddy. "I can do nothing to help him, nothing! I saw him open his arms. Did you see him open his arms?"

Maddy nodded but could not speak. The other elf sang out a black note and made a gesture of assent.

All of the elves were quiet; the frightened twitterings

of the children ceased, the warriors' cries ended. "It is so," the silver-haired elf sighed. "I have heard of this happening. Sometimes a wound can be an invitation to death. I think Sala asked death to come—he knew it was time to leave us and his Lele."

She lifted her head to the sky and let out a long purple note. As she keened, the tree above them dropped all its leaves, which turned silver as they fell. She keened again, and Maddy saw a star streak down the eastern sky. Birds gathered in the bare tree and sang a song so wild and fierce that Maddy could never remember it afterward without shivering and crying.

When the birds' song was done, Lele lifted her head again. Tears streamed down her face, and she cupped them in her hand. She shook her hands, and the silver tears took wing, flying through the air. They circled the head of her dead husband, they circled Maddy and Grandpa, they scribed an arc around the whole band of elves as they knelt mourning, and then the tears darted into the air and disappeared over the trees.

After a silent moment, Lele rose and said something Maddy could not understand. A younger elf came up with a green-and-brown robe decorated with designs of leaves and roots. Gently, Lele wrapped her husband in it, leaving his face clear. Nata and two companions lifted their leader onto one of the largest cats and tied him to the mount.

Nata came and stood by Maddy. He touched her lightly

with one hand, and she jumped. It felt like a butterfly's wing, soft and feathery. "We must go now, Madd-ee. We will take Sala with us and say the final rites for him along the way. We cannot stay here, but must put the place of his death behind us."

Lele stood, looking at Maddy and Grandpa. First she scribed an arc in the air in front of Maddy.

"You, youngling, are full of courage. May it lead you forward on your path. We thank you for your help."

Turning to Grandpa, she circled the air before him. "Old one, I think in a long-ago time you and elves were joined. I can see in your face the mark of an elf from another time. I thought differently from my husband; I believe there *are* humans who can hear our songs."

Grandpa knelt before Lele.

She reached up and gently touched his face. "Someday we may have need of you; sometime you may have need of us. This mark seals the bargain. But you must never speak of it."

Maddy stared at Grandpa but could see nothing. She looked at Nata, standing by Sabrina's head. Maddy started forward, but Grandpa pulled her back.

"Thank you for helping us, old one and youngling." Lele nodded to Maddy and went on. "We must go now. Remember the songs you have heard, and use them to lighten the world."

Turning, she sounded a note on her trumpet, and the

elves walked out of the clearing. As the forest closed behind them, Maddy saw the branches seam together, saw darkness stitch up all the holes so nothing more could be seen of their torches. She clutched Grandpa's arm.

"Nata's gone. I didn't get to say good-bye!" she wailed.

"Hush." Grandpa hugged her. "He had to go, Maddy."

She stared into the forest, watching darkness wash down the trees and branches. Cold lay along her breast, and she began to cry.

Suddenly, Nata burst out of the undergrowth and ran up to her. "Madd-ee, I forgot, with all the grief and shock. I did not say good-bye, and I forgot to give you your name. You have earned your name a thousand times over, by your bravery, by coming here tonight to help us."

She knelt, and he passed his hand over her face. Where he touched, her skin glowed silver. She felt heat, birdsong, and water rushing over her skin. She smelled pines, lemons, and something sweet and unnamed. "Rele, I name you Rele, after the first swordlike grasses that pierce the marsh mud in the spring. Like them, you are sharp and brave. Like them, you seek the sun. Like them, you are full of promise. Go, Rele, and use your gift well. Thank you. And remember, you must never speak of us to anyone."

As Nata turned to go, Maddy called, "Wait! Wait, I have something for you." She reached into her knapsack and drew out the saddle.

He took it from her hand. "Oh, I am happy to have *this* back. Thank you, Rele!"

When he called her name, she heard a rushing sound that reminded her of a falling star speeding across the sky. She watched as he waved and disappeared into the forest.

CHAPTER TWENTY-EIGHT

Maddy stood on the train platform, her bags at her feet. Grandpa stood beside her, arm around her shoulders. He kept giving her little squeezes until she said, "Grandpa! It's all right. I don't mind going back—this time." Always before, at the end of August, they were both crying by the time she got on the train. But this summer, it was different.

"I know, Maddy, I keep expecting to feel sad, but somehow I don't. I keep hearing Nata's song in my ear," Grandpa said, "and it lifts my heart. Strange."

"I know," Maddy said. She peered closely at Grandpa. In the sharp light of early morning, she saw his face more clearly than ever before. The fine lines around his mouth were still there; his eyes were still the same startling blue. His mustache flared out as bravely as ever. But there, just there . . .

"Grandpa! What is this?" She reached up to touch his left cheek, and he grinned.

"I saw it the morning after they left. Didn't you see it before?"

It had only been a week since Nata had gone, but in all that time she hadn't seen the mark. She looked at it again, almost jealous; Grandpa had a sign from the elves, a small crescent moon etched into his cheek, almost hidden by his long white hair. But then she thought, *I have a name. Maybe we each got a different gift.*

"I wonder." She touched the elf sign. A faint tune rose, tinkling and far away.

"I think it means it is not over, not forever, Maddy." Grandpa took her hand, and she gave a little excited jump.

Far away she could see a dark shape moving toward them. The rails rumbled, and people began to gather them-selves on the platform, shifting their bags, straightening their clothes, smoothing their hair.

Maddy looked down. Did she look neat enough? She wore clean jeans and a red shirt, and her hair was combed.

She probably *looked* the same, but neither Mother nor Daddy would know how different she was inside. *Will I ever tell them what happened?*

The train rumbled to a stop, and people spilled out of the cars. Grandpa hugged her tightly and said, "I'm sorry about Sabrina, Maddy."

"So am I," she said into his chest. She guessed she would get used to that sad space inside.

Grandpa sniffed her hair. "I swear, even your hair smells different, Rele." When he used her true name, Maddy suddenly heard all the songs about her: the sand in the cement singing of far beaches, the metal in the rails droning of dark caverns beneath the earth, the clouds overhead whispering of fall and journeys to turquoise seas. A swallow looped over them, and its high, chittering song fell on Maddy. She turned, rubbing her face until her skin shone silver.

"Careful!" Grandpa hid her from the other passengers, wiping her face with the edge of his sleeve. "Don't let *anyone* see, Maddy. Don't sing where people can hear you. They won't understand, and . . . and bad things might happen." He helped her up the steps to the train.

Taking her seat, she watched him climb back down to the platform. The train began to move. She saw him waving, high and sweet and wide in air that was full of birdsong and the promise of fall, and as he waved, she thought for a moment that his ears lengthened and broadened, growing close to his head, and that his face was definitely silver.

The train jerked, her head pressed back against the seat, and the trees and leaves made a green blur outside the window. Maddy sighed and looked out. A barn swallow swooped over the trees, singing:

> *Warm winds go,*
> *cold winds blow.*
> *South in flight*
> *to meadows bright*
> *Good-bye, good-bye.*

GLOSSARY

Aleeno—the elfin word for friend.

Binding Ceremony—when a male and female elf join their lives together for as long as they shall live.

Condine—the first, faint red light of dawn.

Crossing Over—a ceremony where young elves formally achieve adulthood, taking place when they reach eighty years.

Hislin—the silver liquid that flows in elves' veins; can be called elfin "blood." It has healing powers.

The Horned One—a great horned owl who lives in the forest of the elves of the Eastern Woods Clan.

In-gathering—the time in the fall when nuts are harvested and elves gather in their lodges to tell tales.

Joinings—elfin marriages.

Laglan—the elfin word for human beings; not a term of approval.

Lelan—elf bread, baked from the yellow pollen of marsh cattails; nutritious, long-lasting, and often used on journeys.

Mildas—the long story sagas of the elves' past and their brave deeds.

Rele—Maddy's elfin name, referring to the first grasses that pierce the marsh mud in the spring.

Risele—purple-leaved greens that grow in the elves' gardens; rather like lettuce, but with a sharp, bitter taste.

Tileen—the red berries elves feed their cats to make them into more obedient mounts.